"You just have to promise me one thing," Jake said.

Running the pad of her index finger over his tempting bottom lip, her wrist rubbed against the sexy stubble on his cheeks. Her body reacted with a warming shiver. He opened his mouth and gently caught her finger between his teeth. Nipped at it and sucked on it for a moment.

It felt like she'd been waiting her entire life for this moment. Despite his words, he certainly didn't seem to be in a hurry to get away. *Yeah*, he wasn't going anywhere.

Not right now, at least.

"Anything," Anna said.

She wasn't going to let him tell her he wasn't good enough for her.

She knew what she wanted, and he'd just slipped his arms around her again.

"No regrets," he said.

"No regrets," she answered. "But tell me something. How do you know that you're not good for me— that we're not good together—if we've never... tried it out?"

* * *

CELEBRATIONS, INC.: Let's get this party started!

Dear Reader,

In Louisa May Alcott's book *Little Women*, there's a part where she writes about being so scarred by love gone wrong that a person misses out on other—possibly better—chances because of that first bad experience.

Anna Adams, the heroine of *How to Marry a Doctor*, would've saved herself a world of torment if she'd taken to heart that sage advice. Two years after her marriage ended, she wanted to believe in happily-ever-after, but she was too shell-shocked to even date. Still, that didn't stop her from trying to fix up her lifelong best friend, Jake Lennox, with the "right kind of woman" (to end the parade of beautiful women who were hopelessly wrong for him). Jake countered: if Anna would let him fix her up, he'd let her fix him up. In fact, the first one to introduce the other to a person who stuck was the winner. It sounded like a good plan...until they finally realized the reason none of the dates were working out was because they were much happier in each other's company.

I hope you enjoy Jake and Anna's story as much as I enjoyed writing it. Please look me up on Facebook at facebook.com/nancyrobardsthompsonbooks, or drop me a line at nrobardsthompson@yahoo.com.

Warmly,

Nancy Robards Thompson

How to Marry a Doctor

Nancy Robards Thompson

Recycling programs
for this product may
not exist in your area.

ISBN-13: 978-0-373-65898-5

How to Marry a Doctor

Copyright © 2015 by Nancy Robards Thompson

Printed in U.S.A.

National bestselling author **Nancy Robards Thompson** holds a degree in journalism. She worked as a newspaper reporter until she realized reporting "just the facts" bored her silly. Much more content to report to her muse, Nancy loves writing women's fiction and romance full-time. Critics have deemed her work "funny, smart and observant." She resides in Florida with her husband and daughter. You can reach her at nancyrobardsthompson.com and facebook.com/nancyrobardsthompsonbooks.

Books by Nancy Robards Thompson

Harlequin Special Edition

Celebrations, Inc.

A Celebration Christmas
Celebration's Baby
Celebration's Family
Celebration's Bride
Texas Christmas
Texas Magic
Texas Wedding

The Fortunes of Texas: Cowboy Country

My Fair Fortune

**The Fortunes of Texas:
Welcome to Horseback Hollow**

Falling for Fortune

The Fortunes of Texas: Whirlwind Romance

Fortune's Unexpected Groom

The Baby Chase

The Family They Chose

Accidental Heiress
Accidental Father
Accidental Cinderella
Accidental Princess

Visit the Author Profile page at Harlequin.com for more titles.

This book is dedicated to
everyone who believes in happily ever after.

Chapter One

Anna Adams parked her yellow VW Beetle in Jake Lennox's driveway, grabbed her MP3 player and took a moment to make sure it was loaded and ready to go.

She was about to hold an intervention and music—just the right song—was the key component of this quirky job.

Today, she was going to save Jake, her lifelong best friend, from himself. Or at least from drowning in the quicksand of his own sorrow.

This morning, Celebration Memorial Hospital had been abuzz with rumors that Jake's girlfriend, Dorenda, had dumped him. Anna might've been a little miffed that she'd had to hear about his breakup through the nursing staff grapevine, but the sister of one of Dorenda's friends was an LPN who worked the seven-to-three shift at the hospital and she'd come in positively brimming over with the gossip.

Jake had been scarce today. He hadn't been around for lunch. Another doctor had done rounds today. When she'd tried to phone Jake after work, the call had gone to voice mail.

The radio silence was what made Anna worry. She hadn't realized that he'd been so hung up on *Miss Texas*. That's what everyone called Dorenda, even though no one was sure if she'd actually held the title or if she'd gotten the nickname simply because she was tall and beautiful and looked like she should've worn a crown to her day job. Poor schlubs like Anna did well to make it to their shifts at the hospital wearing mascara and lipstick.

Anna wasn't sure what the real story was. When Jake had a girlfriend, he tended to disappear into the tunnel of love. Or at least he never seemed to bring his girlfriends around her. And Dr. Jake Lennox usually had a girlfriend.

Anna didn't celebrate Jake's breakups, but she had to admit she did relish the intervals between his relationships, because, for as long as she'd known him, that was when she'd gotten her friend back. Sure, they usually saw each other daily at the hospital. It was not as if he completely disappeared. But in those times between relationships, he always gravitated to her.

She would take the spaces in between any day. Because those spaces ran deeper than the superficial stretches of time he spent with the Miss Texases of the world.

Anna rapped their special knock—*knock, knock-knock, knock, knock*—on Jake's front door, then let herself in.

He never locked the door, but then again, they never waited to be invited into each other's homes. "Jake? Are you here?"

Really, she wasn't surprised when he didn't answer. In fact, she had a pretty good idea of where he was. So, she closed the door and let herself in the backyard gate and followed the mulch path down to the lake, the crowning jewel of his property.

Yep, if he was back here brooding, it clearly called for an intervention or, as they'd come to call it over the years, the Sadness Intervention Dance.

It was their private ritual. Whenever one of them was blue about something, the other performed the dumbest dance he or she could come up with for the sole reason of making the other person smile. The dance was always different, but the song was *always* the same: "Don't Worry, Be Happy" by Bobby McFerrin.

Jake had invented it way back in elementary school. Gosh, it was so long ago—back when the song had just hit the airwaves—she couldn't even remember what she'd been upset about that had compelled him to make a fool of himself to jolt her out of it. But it stuck and stayed with them over the years and now, even though they were both in their thirties, it was still their ritual. The SID was as much a part of them as all those New Year's Eves their families had rung in together or all those Fourths of July at the lake they'd shared. Back in the day, the mere gesture was always enough to push the recipient out of his or her funk. Or, on the rare occasion that it didn't, the SID was the kickoff of the pity party and the guest of honor was officially put on notice that he or she had exactly twenty-four hours to get over whatever was bringing him or her down. Because whatever it was, it wasn't worth the wasted emotion.

Nowadays, it was usually performed at the end of a love affair, as was the case today and the time that Jake had basically saved her life when her marriage had ended—metaphorically speaking, of course. But then again, he was a doctor. Saving lives was second nature to him.

Love was no longer second nature to Anna.

Sure, once upon a time, she'd believed in true love.

She'd believed in the big white dress and the happily-ever-after. She'd believed in spending Saturday nights snuggling on the couch, watching a movie with her husband. She'd believed in her wedding vows, especially the part where they'd said *'til death do us part* and *forsaking all others*. From that day forward, the promises she and Hal had made were etched on her soul.

Then it all exploded right in front of her face.

After nearly four years of marriage, she discovered Hal, who had also looked her in the eyes and made the same vows on their wedding day, had been sleeping with his office manager.

That was when Anna had stopped believing in just about everything. Well, everything except for the one person in the world who had ever been true to her: Jake Lennox.

Jake had been her first friend, her first kiss, and the

first guy to stick around after they realized they were much better friends than anything more.

He'd never stopped believing in her.

After finding out about Hal's infidelity, the only thing Anna had wanted to do was to numb the pain with pints of Ben and Jerry's and curl up into the fetal position in between feedings. Jake, however, was having none of that. He'd arrived on her doorstep in San Antonio and pulled her out of her emotional sinkhole and set her back on her feet. Then one month ago, after the divorce was final, he'd come back to San Antonio, single-handedly packed Anna's belongings and moved her to Celebration. He'd even helped her find a house and had gotten her a nursing job at Celebration Memorial Hospital.

But before he'd done any of this, he'd done the SID.

There he stood: a tall, handsome thirty-four-year-old man doing the most ridiculous dance you could ever imagine to "Don't Worry, Be Happy."

Was it any wonder that Anna felt duty-bound to be there for him on a day like today?

It was her turn to perform the SID. As humiliating as it was—well, that was the point. Anna was fully prepared to make a colossal fool of herself.

The gardenia bushes were in full bloom. Their heady scent mixed with the earthy smell of the lake perfuming the humid evening air. She swatted away a mosquito who had decided she was dinner.

Instinct told her she'd find Jake on the dock, most likely sitting on the ground with his feet in the water and a beer in his hand. Her intuition didn't let her down.

There he sat, with his back to her, exactly as she had imagined. His lanky body was silhouetted by the setting sun. She could just make out his too-long brown hair that looked a little mussed, as if he'd recently raked his fingers through it. He was clad in blue jeans and a mint-green polo shirt. A symphony of cicadas supplied the sound track to the sunset, which had painted the western sky into an Impressionistic masterpiece in shades of orange, pink and blue.

A gentle wind stirred, rippling the lake water and providing welcome relief to the oppressive heat.

Obviously, Jake hadn't heard her coming.

Good. The element of surprise always helped with the SID.

She took advantage of the moment to ready herself, drawing in a couple of deep breaths and doing some shoulder rolls. With one last check of the volume on her MP3 player, she pushed Play and Bobby McFerrin's whistling reggae strains preempted the cicadas' night song.

Jake's head whipped around the minute he heard the music. Then he turned the rest of his body toward her, giving her his full attention.

Anna sprang into action attempting to do something she hoped resembled the moonwalk. Thank goodness she didn't have to watch herself and the shameless lengths she was going to tonight.

Once she'd maneuvered off the grass and was dancing next to him on the dock, she broke into alternate moves that were part robot and part Charleston and part something…er…original.

As she danced, trying her best to coax a full-on smile from him, she tried to ignore the sinking feeling that maybe he'd been more serious about Dorenda than the others. That his most current ex had sent him into a Texas-sized bad humor.

She reminded herself that was exactly why she was here today. For some quality time with her best bud. To bring him out of his post-breakup funk. She knew she looked ridiculous in her pink nurse's scrubs that were slightly too big and clunky white lace-up shoes, but Jake's initial scowl was beginning to morph into a lopsided smile, despite himself. She could actually see him trying to fight it.

Oh, yeah, he was fighting it, but he couldn't fool her. She knew him much too well.

In fact, it only made her unleash the most ridiculous of her dance moves: the sprinkler, the cotton-swab, and the Running Man. Dignity drew the line at dropping down onto her stomach and doing the worm. Although that move hadn't been below Jake a month ago when he'd been there after she'd signed her divorce papers.

That intervention had been a doozy and a true testament to the depth of their friendship.

But he wouldn't have to perform another intervention for her anytime soon.

After losing herself and getting burned so badly, Anna wasn't in any hurry to get involved again.

For now, she was happy to serve as Jake's intervener. *Sprinkler*-two-three-four, *cotton-swab*-two-three-four, *Running Man*-two-three… She was just getting into a groove, ready to transition from the Running

Man back to the robot when, in the middle of possibly the best sequence yet, her foot hit an uneven plank on the dock, causing her to lose her balance.

She saw the fall coming in slow motion and she would have face-planted if not for Jake's quick reflexes. Instead of kissing the dock, she found herself safe in the strength of his strong arms, looking up into his gorgeous blue eyes.

Anna smelled good.

The kind of *natural good* that made him want to pull her closer, bury his face in her neck and breathe in deeply.

But this was *Anna*, for God's sake.

He couldn't do that.

He respected her too much and owed her so much more than that.

Especially after she'd gone to such crazy lengths to cheer him up. Did he dare tell her that he really didn't need cheering up? Not in the way she thought he did. Sure, Dorenda had ended things, but the breakup had come as more of a relief than anything.

Before he did something stupid that would be awkward for both Anna and him, he set her upright and took a step back, allowing both of them to reclaim their personal space.

"That was graceful," he said, hoping humor would help him regain his equilibrium.

"You know me," Anna said. "Grace is my middle name." Actually, it really was. "I aim to please. How are you doing, Jake? You okay?"

Her long auburn hair hung at her shoulders in loose waves. Her clear, ivory skin was virtually makeup-free. She had this look in her blue eyes that warmed him from the inside out.

He tried not to think about the strange impulse he'd had just a minute ago, an impulse that lingered even if he was trying not to acknowledge it.

"I'm great," he said. "Want a beer? I'd like to toast your latest choreography. You're getting really good at it. I'll give your Running Man a nine-point-five. I have to take off a half point since you didn't stick the landing."

She swatted him and quickly crossed her arms in front of her.

"Yes, I'd love a beer. Thank you. I need one after that."

He smiled. "Come on. Let's go back up to the house. I have five of a six-pack in the fridge."

She was eyeing him again. "Well, good. I was afraid that maybe you'd been at home all day drowning your sorrows."

"I was seeing patients all day. In case you haven't noticed, I usually don't take off midweek to go on a bender."

He and Anna both worked at Celebration Memorial Hospital, but she was an OB nurse on the third-floor maternity ward and he was a hospitalist on the general medical-surgical floors. Unless they sought each other out, their paths usually didn't cross at work.

"I must say, you're taking this awfully well," she said.

"What?"

"The breakup. If I didn't know better, I'd swear that you were fine."

"Do I act like I'm not fine?"

"Well, no. That's what I just said. You seem remarkably unfazed by Miss Texas's departure. Sorry, by *Dorenda's* breaking up with you."

He pulled open the back door for her and stepped aside so she could enter the house first.

"Dorenda was a great woman, but our relationship had run its course. I'll miss her, but it was time to move on."

He shrugged and stepped inside behind her.

"Are you telling me that *you* broke up with *her*?"

Throwing her a glance over his shoulder as he walked toward the kitchen, he said, "No, she's the one who dropped the bomb. Actually, it was more of an exploding ultimatum. I saw it coming a mile away."

He reached into the fridge, grabbed a beer and twisted off the bottle cap.

"She gave you an ultimatum? Really? Well, but then again, how long were the two of you together?"

"Four or five months or so. Do you want a mug? I have some in the freezer."

"Yes, please. Had it really been five months? I mean, I've only been back a month."

He nodded as he poured the beer down the inside of the mug, careful to create just the right amount of foam on top. "She reminded me of that more than a few times last night. She was talking five-year plans that involved marriage and kids and bigger houses. She kept saying she needed some assurance about our future, needed to know where we were going. I'm not going to lie to her. I enjoyed her company, but I wasn't going to marry her."

He handed the beer to Anna.

"Why not?" Anna asked. "She was beautiful. You seemed like you were really into her."

Jake nodded. "She was nice. Pretty. But...I couldn't see myself spending the rest of my life with her. That's the bottom line."

Anna squinted at him, her brows drawn together, as she sipped her beer.

"What's wrong? Is the beer not good? You don't have to drink it if you don't like it."

She set down the mug on the kitchen counter. "No, I like it. But I have two questions for you."

"Okay. Shoot."

"First question. If you're *fine* with everything, how come you let me keep dancing and make a fool of myself?"

Her voice was stern.

He laughed out loud. He couldn't help it. "Are you kidding? Watching you was the most fun I've had in months. No way was I going to stop you. For the record, you didn't make a fool of yourself. You're adorable. In fact, you'd been away so long down there in San Antonio, I'd almost forgotten how adorable you are."

She rolled her eyes, but then smiled.

"So happy to have cheered you up," she said.

"What's the second question?" he asked.

She looked at him thoughtfully for a long moment.

"Why, Jake? Why do you keep dating the same type of women? I don't mean to be judgmental and I know I haven't been around for the last decade or so. But think of this as tough love. You keep dating the same type of women, expecting to get different results, but it always turns out the same way. Always has, always will."

He crossed his arms, feeling a little defensive, but knowing she was right. Sometimes her friendship felt like the only real thing in the world. But still, he didn't want to get into this right now.

"I don't exactly see you out there blazing trails in the dating world," he countered.

She sighed. "The divorce has only been final for a month."

"But you were separated for nearly two years."

"This isn't about me, Jake. This is about you. What are you looking for?"

He shook his head.

"*Company.* Companionship? That's why, when I know the relationship has run its course, I end it. Or in today's case, I let Dorenda do the honors. I don't string them along."

"But you do sort of string them along. You dated Dorenda for four months. That's a significant amount of time in the post-twenties dating world."

Overhead, the fluorescent lights buzzed. He glanced out the kitchen window. Inky dusk was blotting out the last vestiges of the sunset.

"I don't know what you want me to say, Anna."

"Say that you'll let me fix you up with a different type of woman."

Different?

"Define *different*."

"Don't take this the wrong way, but maybe you should consider women who are a little more down-to-earth than the Miss Texases of the world."

He knocked back the last of his beer and debated grabbing another, but his stomach growled, reminding him he really should think about getting some food into his system first.

"Down-to-earth, huh? I wouldn't even know where to begin to look for someone down-to-earth."

"Exactly. That's why I want you to let me fix you up."

"I don't know, Anna. Blind dates aren't really my thing."

He returned to the fridge, pulled open the door and surveyed the meager contents.

"When was the last time you went on a blind date?"

"Better question," he countered. "When was the last time *you* even went on a date?"

He looked back over his shoulder to gauge her reaction. She didn't seem to like being in the line of fire any more than he did.

"This isn't about me, Jake."

"It's been nearly two years since you and Hal broke up. So, while we're on the subject, it's high time for *you* to get back in the saddle and try again."

She put her hands on her hips and shook her head, looking solemn. "Okay, you're changing the subject, and I don't know if I even want to date. You, on the other hand, obviously do like getting involved. I know you so well, and if you'll just let me help you, I'll bet I can make it a much more rewarding experience for you. Or at least one that has the potential to last, maybe even change your mind about marriage. Come on. Be a sport."

"Why are women always trying to change me?"

"The right woman wouldn't change you, but she might make you want to see other possibilities.

He took out a carton of eggs, some butter, various veggies and the vestiges of a package of turkey bacon. It was all he had. When all else failed, breakfast for dinner always worked. It was his favorite go-to meal when the pickings were slim. He really should go to the grocery store later tonight. The rest of his week was busy.

"You'd really wager that you could fix me up with someone who is better for me than my usual type?"

She raised her chin. "You bet I could. In fact, I'll bet I could introduce you to your soul mate if you gave me a fair chance."

He chuckled. "You are the eternal optimist. Do you want to stay for dinner? I'll make us an omelet."

She put her hand on her stomach. "That sounds great. I'm starving. We can talk more about this wager. How can I help with dinner?"

"You can wash and dice the onions and red peppers."

She stepped up to the sink to prep the peppers, but first she began by putting some dirty dishes into the dishwasher and hand-washed several pieces of flatware.

"You don't have to do that," he said. "I didn't have time to clean up this morning before I left for work. I'll do those later when I clean up the dinner dishes."

"Actually, it's sort of hard to wash the peppers with dishes in the way. I don't mind, really. You are fixing me dinner. And we're going to need forks to eat with."

Jake left her to do what she needed to do because God knew she would anyway.

He took a bowl out of one of the cupboards and began cracking eggs into it. "Since when did you become a matchmaker? And what makes you think you can find me the right woman? I've been trying all these years and I haven't been successful."

"That's easy. A—I know you better than you know yourself, and B—you are attracted to the wrong women. Your judgment is clouded. Mine is not."

She might've had a point. But after just getting out of a relationship, he wasn't very eager to jump back into anything serious. So looking at it from that perspective, what harm would a few dates do? Other than take up what little free time he had away from the hospital. He could indulge Anna. She meant that much to him. Then again, could he ever really expect to find his soul mate or anyone long-term when he never wanted to get married?

That was something he'd known for as long as he'd had a sense of himself as an adult. He did not want to get married. Marriage was the old ball and chain. It took something good, a relationship where two people chose to be together, and turned it into a contractual obligation. He'd witnessed it firsthand with his parents. All he could remember was the fighting, his mom leaving and his father's profound sadness. Sadness that drove him to seek solace in the bottle. Anna knew his family history. Sure, she'd have good intentions. She'd think she was steering him toward someone who made him happy, but what was the point?

Jake vowed he'd never give a woman that much power over him.

So he said, "Before we go any farther, I have a stipulation."

"Jake, no. If we're going to do this and do it right, you have to play by my rules. You can't give me a laundry list of what you want. That's where you get into trouble with all these preconceived notions. Maybe we can talk about deal breakers, such as must not be marriage-minded or must not want kids, etcetera, but we're not getting into the superficial. You're just going to have to trust me."

He poured a little milk into the eggs, a shake of salt, a grind of black pepper and began to beat them. Even though they'd spent a lot of time apart, Anna still knew him so well. A strange warmth spread through him and he whisked the eggs a little faster to work off the weird sensation.

"I wasn't going to get superficial. In fact, my stipulation wasn't even about me. I want to propose a double wager. Since we both need dates to the Holbrook wedding, I'll let you fix me up, if you'll let me fix you up."

The daughter of Celebration Memorial Hospital's chief executive officer Stanley Holbrook was getting married in mid-July. Jake had his eye on a promotion and attending his boss's daughter's wedding was one of the best ways to prove to the man he was the guy for the job. Since Holbrook was a conservative family man, Anna's offer to fix him up with a woman of substance wasn't a bad idea.

She was looking at him funny.

"Deal?" he said.

She opened her mouth, but then clamped it shut before saying anything. Instead, she shook her head. "No. Just...*no*."

"Come on, Anna, fair is fair. I know Hal hurt you, but you're too young to put yourself on a shelf. You want to get married again. You want to have kids. There are good guys out there, and I think I know one or two who would be worthy of you."

She stopped chopping. "Worthy of me?" Her expression softened. "That's the sweetest thing anyone has said to me in a very long time."

"Case in point of why you need to get out more, my dear. Men should be saying many *nice* things to you."

She made short order of chopping the peppers, scraping the tiny pieces into a bowl and then drying her hands.

"Okay, I'll make a deal with you," she said. "We'll do this until Stan Holbrook's daughter's wedding. Between now and then, I'll bet I can match you with your soul mate and cure you of your serial monogamy issues."

He winced. "What? As in something permanent?"

She shrugged. "Just give me a chance."

"Only if you'll let me do the same for you. Do we have a deal?"

She nodded.

"So what are we betting?"

She shrugged. "I didn't really mean it as a serious bet."

"I think making a bet will make this more interesting. We don't have to decide the prize right away. Let's just agree that the first one who succeeds in making a match for the other wins."

Anna wrinkled her nose. "Knowing you, you'll let a good woman go just to win the challenge. You're so competitive."

"But if you think about it," he said, "who will be the real winner? One will win the bet, but the other will win love."

"That's extremely profound for a man who has such bad taste in women." She gave him that smile that always made him feel as if he'd come home. He paused to just take it in for a moment.

Then Jake shook her smooth, warm hand, and said, "Here's to soul mates."

Chapter Two

*S*oul *mates*.

Why did hearing Jake say that word make her stomach flip? Especially since she wasn't even sure if she believed in such a thing as *soul mates*. After all she'd been through with Hal, she still believed in love and marriage enough to try again…someday. But *soul mates*? That was an entirely different subject. The sparkle had dulled from that notion when her marriage died.

"I'm done chopping." Anna set the bowl on the granite counter next to the stove where Jake was melting butter in a frying pan. Then she deposited their empty beer bottles into the recycle bin in the garage.

"Now what can I do?" she said when she got back into the kitchen.

"Just have a seat over there." With his elbow, he gestured toward the small kitchen table cluttered with mail and books. "Stay out of my way. Omelet-flipping is serious business. I am a trained professional. So don't try this at home."

"I wouldn't dream of it," she said, eyeing the mess on the table's surface. "That's why I have you. So you can fix me omelets. Apparently, I will repay you by setting the table for us to eat. And after I've excavated a space to put the plates and silverware, then I might clean the rest of your house, too. I thought you had a housekeeper. Where has she been?"

"Her name's Angie and she's been down with the flu. Hasn't been available to come in for two weeks."

Anna glanced around the room at the newspapers littering the large, plush sectional sofa in the open-plan living room. There were mugs and stacks of magazines and opened mail on the masculine, wooden coffee and end tables. Several socks and running shoes littered the dark-stained, hardwood living room floor.

"Wow. Well…" In fact, it looked as if Jake had dropped everything right where he'd stood. "God, Jake, I didn't realize you were such a slob."

Jake followed her gaze. "I'm not a slob," he said. "I'm just busy. And I wasn't expecting company."

Obviously.

Anna thought about asking why he didn't simply walk a few more steps into the bathroom where he could deposit his socks into the dirty clothes hamper rather than leaving them strewn all over the floor. Instead, she focused on being part of the solution rather than nagging him and adding to the problem. She quickly organized the table clutter into neat piles, revealing two placemats underneath, and set out the silverware she'd just washed and dried.

"Where are your napkins?" she asked.

He handed her a roll of paper towels.

This was the first time in the month that she'd been home that they'd cooked at his place. Really, it was just an impromptu meal, but it was just dawning on her how little she'd been over at his place since she'd been back. That was thanks in large part to Jake's girlfriend. She wondered if Dorenda had seen the mess—or had helped create it—but before she could ask, she realized she really didn't want to know.

"It must be a pretty serious case of the flu if Angie has been down for *two* weeks. Has she been to the doctor?"

Jake gave a one-shoulder shrug. "She's fine. I ran into her at the coffee shop in downtown the other day. She looked okay to me. She'll probably be back next week."

Anna balked. "Why do you keep her?"

She crossed the room to straighten the newspapers and corral the socks. She couldn't just stand there while Jake was cooking and the papers were cluttering up the place and in the back of her mind she could hear him toasting soul mates.

Even that small act of picking up would help work off some of her nervous energy.

"I don't have time to find someone else," he said. "Besides, it's not that bad around here."

She did a double take, looking back at him to see if he was kidding.

Apparently not.

But even if it looked as if Jake had simply dropped things and left them where they fell, the house wasn't dirty. It didn't smell bad. In fact, it smelled like *him*— like coffee and leather and something else that bridged the years and swept her back to a simpler time before she'd married the wrong man and Jake had become a serial monogamist. She breathed in deeper, wondering if they were still the same people or if the years and circumstances had changed them too much.

She bent to pick up a dog-eared issue of *Sports Illustrated* that was sprawled on the floor facedown. As she prepared to close it back to its regular shape, she nearly dropped it again when she spied the tiny, silky purple thong hidden underneath. Like a lavender spider. Only it didn't get up and crawl away.

"Eww." Anna grimaced. "I think Miss Texas forgot something."

Jake gave a start as his gaze fell to where Anna pointed.

She reached over and grabbed the poker from the fireplace tool set on the hearth and used it to lift the thong off the ground.

"This is classy. How does a woman forget her underwear?"

He smiled that adorable lopsided smile that always suggested something a little bit naughty. There was no doubt why women fell for him. Heck, she'd fall for him if he weren't her best friend.

"She carried a big purse," Jake said. "It was like a

portable closet. She probably didn't leave here com-mando." His gaze strayed back to the panties. "Then again, maybe she did."

Anna raised the poker. The thong resembled a scanty purple flag, which she swiftly disposed of in the trash can.

"She might want that back," Jake protested.

"Really? You think she's going to call and ask if you found her underwear?"

They locked gazes.

"If she does—" Anna scowled at him and pointed to the garbage "—it's right here."

He was quiet as he pulled out the toaster and put in two slices of whole wheat bread.

Anna returned the poker to its stand.

"Jake, this is why we need to have a heart-to-heart talk about what you want in a woman. It's no won-der you can't seriously consider spending the rest of your life with a woman who leaves her panties on your living room floor. Even if she lived here, *leaving* her panties lying around in the living room wouldn't be a good sign."

"I leave my socks on the floor," he said as he trans-ferred the omelet from the frying pan onto the two plates Anna had set out.

"Yeah, and it wouldn't take that much more effort to put them in the laundry hamper," she said. "Do you want orange juice? I need orange juice with my eggs."

"Sorry, I'm out. I have coffee and there's more beer. I need to go to the grocery store. I really should go tonight because I'm not going to have time to go later with everything going on this weekend."

She passed on the beer. Not her favorite thing to drink with eggs. Even if it was dinner. It was one of those combos that just didn't sound appetizing. She opted for making herself a quick cup of coffee in his single-serving coffee brewer. As she pushed the button selecting the serving size, it dawned on her that even if they had been apart for a long time, she still felt at home with Jake. She could raid his K-Cups and brew herself a cup without asking. Even in the short amount of time that she'd spent here, she knew which cabinet contained the coffee, and that he stored his dinner plates in the lower cabinet to the right of the sink because they stacked better there.

"I need some groceries, too," she said. "How about if we shop together after we do the dishes? We can talk as we shop and figure out where the happy medium is between the nice women you *should* be dating and the ones who leave their underwear all over town."

Jake's brows knit together as he set the dinner plates on the table.

"Don't look at me like that," Anna said as she slid into her seat at the table. "You know I'm right. If you keep doing what you're doing, you'll keep getting what you're getting and you'll keep repeating the same pattern. You need to look a little deeper than a pretty face."

He sat down, speared some of the omelet and took a bite, watching her as he chewed. She wished he'd say something. Not with food in his mouth, of course. But that was the thing about Jake—he may be a manly guy's guy who didn't know how to pick up after himself, but he still had manners. He didn't talk with his mouth full, he said please and thank-you; Jake Lennox was a gentleman.

He knew how to treat a lady. He just didn't know how to choose the right lady.

"So what are the deal breakers, Jake?"

"Deal breakers?"

"You know, the qualities in a woman that you can't live with."

"Why don't we focus on the good? The attributes that I'm attracted to?"

"Because attraction is what gets you in trouble. Attraction is what caused Miss Texas to leave her thong on your living room floor."

Ugh. She sounded like such a harpy. She knew that even before she saw the look on his face and consciously softened her tone.

"I don't mean to be a nag. Really, I don't. It's just that sometimes it helps if you work backward."

She wasn't going to pressure him. That was the fastest way to suck all the fun out of the bet. This was supposed to be *fun*, not an exercise in browbeating.

She was prepared to change the subject when he said, "Anyone I date has to be comfortable with the fact that I don't want to get married and I don't want kids. I don't want anyone who thinks they can change my mind. That's a deal breaker. It's what started things going south with Dorenda. She was Miss Independent for the first couple of months. Then she started in with the *five-year plan*, which eventually turned into an ultimatum."

Anna realized it was the first time she'd ever been on Dorenda's side. Who could blame her for wanting more? Especially when it involved more Jake. But she wasn't going to argue with him. This anti-marriage/anti-family stance was new. Or at least something that had developed during the time that they were apart. Probably the reason he'd been involved in his string of relationships. Jake had grown up in a single-parent household. His mom had left the family when Jake was in first grade.

One night before they left for college, when she and Jake were having one of their famous heart-to-hearts, he'd opened up about how hard it had been on him and his brothers when their mom left the family.

Yet he'd never mentioned that he didn't want to get married.

Actually, though, when she thought about it, it was a good thing he was being so up front about everything. That's just how Jake was. He knew himself, and he was true to himself. Maybe if Hal had been more honest with both of them, they might have avoided a world of hurt.

So yeah, considering *that*, Jake's candid admission was a good thing.

Now, her mind and its deductive reasoning just had to convince her heart that was true, because she hated the thought of Jake ending up alone years down the road.

"So you want someone who is family-oriented, funny, kind, honest and smart," Jake recapped as he pushed the shopping cart down the canned goods aisle in the grocery store. "You don't want to date a doctor, because of Hal. So what about looks? What's your type?"

Anna stopped to survey a row of black beans lined up like soldiers on a shelf.

"I thought we agreed that we weren't going to concentrate on the physical. That's where we get into trouble. We need to get past that."

"What? Should I disqualify a guy if he is good-looking?"

She quirked a brow at him as she set two cans in the otherwise empty cart. "I'd love to hear your idea of a good-looking guy."

He scowled back at her. "I don't know. Beauty is in the eye of the beholder, as they say. I have no idea what makes a guy attractive to a woman."

"I was just teasing, Jake. You know you're my ideal. If I can't have you, then…"

She made a *tsk*ing sound and squeezed his arm as she walked farther down the aisle to get something else on her list.

If he didn't know her so well, he might've thought her harmless flirtation had started a ripple of *something* inside him. But that was utterly ridiculous. This was *Anna*, and that's why he couldn't put his finger on the *something* she'd stirred. Maybe it was pride, or actually, more like gratitude that pulled at him. He looked at her in her scrubs that were a little too big for her slight frame. Her purse, which she'd slung across her body, proved that there were curves hidden away under all that pink fabric.

He averted his gaze, because *this was Anna.* Dammit, he shouldn't be looking at her as if she was something he'd ask the butcher to put on a foam tray and wrap up in cellophane. As the thought occurred to him, he realized his gaze had meandered back to where it had no business straying.

He turned his body away from her and toward the shelf of black beans Anna had just pored over. He didn't know what the hell to do with canned black beans, but he took a couple of cans and added them to the cart as he warred with the very real realization that he didn't want to fix her up with just anyone. Certainly not most of his buddies, who if they talked about Anna the way they talked about other women he'd have no choice but to deck.

"Excuse me." Jake looked over to see a small, silver-haired woman holding out a piece of paper. "Your wife dropped this list." The woman hooked her thumb in Anna's direction at the other end of the aisle. "I'd go give it to her myself, but I'm going this way."

My wife?

Jake smiled at the woman and started to correct her, to explain that he and Anna weren't married, but the words seemed to stick in his throat. He found himself reaching out and accepting the paper—a grocery list— and saying, "Thanks, I'll give it to her."

She nodded and was on her way before Jake could say anything else.

Hmm. My wife.

He tried to see what the woman saw—Anna and him together…as a couple. But in similar fashion to not being able to look at her curves in good conscience, he couldn't fully let his mind go there.

It wasn't that the thought disgusted him—or anything negative like that. On the contrary. And that brought a whole host of other weirdness with it. The only way around it was to laugh it off.

"You dropped your list," he said as he stopped the cart next to her. "The nice lady who found it thought you were my wife."

Anna shot him a dubious look. "Oh, yeah? Did you set her straight?"

She deposited more canned goods into the basket and then took the list from his hand.

"No. I didn't. I need bread. Which aisle is the bread in?"

She let the issue drop. He almost wished she would've said something snide like, *That's awkward.* Or, *Me? Married to you? Never in a million years.* Instead, she changed the subject. "Do you want bakery bread or prepackaged? And why don't you know where the bread is?"

He certainly didn't dwell on it.

"I don't know. I guess I don't retain that kind of information. Grocery shopping isn't my favorite sport."

"I can tell," she said. "And if you don't pick up the pace, you're going to get a penalty for delay of game. I'm almost finished. Where's your list? Let me see if I can help move this along."

"I don't have a list," he said. He knew he should make an off-the-cuff comment about her, his pretend wife, being the keeper of the list for both of them, but it didn't feel right.

Since when had anything ever not felt right with Anna?

"I keep the list in my head," he added.

"And of course, you're out of everything. Here, I can help. We'll just grab things for you as we go by them."

She pulled the shopping cart from the front end and turned the corner into the next aisle.

"Do you want cereal?" she asked.

Before he could answer, a couple a few feet away from them broke out into an argument that silenced both Anna and him.

"Look, I'm an adult," said the guy. "If I want to eat sugary cereal for breakfast, I will. In fact, if I want to eat a bowl of pure sugar, I will. You get what you like and I'll get what I want."

"Breakfast is the most important meal of the day, honey." The woman took a cereal box—the bright yellow kind with fake berries—out of the shopping cart and put it back on the shelf. "This won't hold you. You need something with fiber and protein. If you eat this, you'll be raiding the vending machine by ten o'clock."

The guy took the cereal box off the shelf and put it back in the cart. "I grew up eating this stuff. You're my wife, not the food police. So hop off."

Anna and Jake quickened their pace as they passed the couple. They exchanged a look, which the couple obviously didn't notice because now insults were inching their way into the exchange and tones were getting heated.

"We'll come back for cereal," Anna said.

Jake nodded. "When we do, are you going to mock my cereal choice?"

"Why would I do that? I'm not your wife."

There. Good. She said it. The dreaded w word.

"Are you saying it's a wife's role to mock her husband's cereal choice?"

"Of course not. I never told Hal what he could and couldn't eat. Then again, since I was the one who cooked in that relationship, he didn't have much say. But he was completely on his own for breakfast and lunch, free to make his own choices. And you see where that got me. Do you think we would've lasted if I had been more concerned?"

"No. Hal was an ass. He didn't deserve your picking out healthy cereal for him."

"So you're saying the woman picking out the cereal rather than leaving him to his own devices was a good thing?"

"Well, yeah. For the record, in the couple we saw back there, the wife was right. He may have wanted that crap, but he didn't need it. So I'll side with her. Do you want me to go back over there and tell her I'm on her side?"

"Better not. Not if you want to keep all your teeth."

Jake laughed but it sounded bitter—even to his own ears. "Why does that have to happen in relationships? People get married and end up hating each other over the most ridiculous things. They fight and tear each other apart and someone leaves. That marriage is in trouble over Much-n-Crunch and its artificially flavored berries. That's exactly why I don't want marriage."

"So you're saying that the guy should've gotten the cereal he wanted?"

"No. I already said I thought the wife was right. Junk like that *will* kill you. I agree with her. Healthy eating habits are good."

As they strolled past the dairy section, Anna studied him for a minute. "I've just figured out who I'm fixing you up with on your first date. She's a nutritionist. I think the two of you will have a lot in common. I can't believe I didn't think of her until now."

Her response caught him off guard.

"What is she like?" he asked.

Anna raised her brows. "You'll just have to wait and see."

"Okay. Two can play that game," he said. "You'll have to be surprised on your first date, too."

She grimaced. "Go easy on me, Jake. I'm so out of practice. You know how I am. I'm casual. I haven't been out there in so long."

"That's why you need me to fix you up."

He had no idea who he was going to pick for her first date. Who would be worthy of her? Maybe the best place for him to start would be to rule out anyone who was remotely similar to himself. Because Anna deserved so much better.

Chapter Three

"Try this one." Anna's sister, Emily, shoved a royal blue sundress with a white Indian motif on the front through the opening in the fitting room curtain in the Three Sisters dress shop in downtown Celebration. "It looks like the basis of a good first-date outfit."

Anna still wasn't sure who her date was or where they were going, but one thing she did know was they were getting together on Wednesday and she had nothing to wear. It had been so long since she'd worn anything but jeans or hospital scrubs, she didn't have a stitch appropriate for a…date. Plus, she had a busy week ahead and this was Emily's night off. So Anna figured she might as well seize the moment and bring her sister along to help her pick out something nice. If she felt good with what she was wearing, she might feel less nervous on the date, thereby eliminating one potential avenue of stress…or disaster.

She held up the dress her sister had chosen and looked at herself in the mirror. The white pattern running up the front of the dress had a design that might've made a nice henna tattoo. It was a little wild for her taste.

"I don't know, Em, this one looks a little low cut."

"Try it on. You never can tell when it's on the hanger."

Wasn't that the truth? The same rule could apply to men, too. You had to try them on—well, not literally, of course. She couldn't fathom getting intimate with a man. Even if it was a man Jake had picked out for her. Not that she was contemplating life as a born-again virgin. It was just too much to contemplate right now. First, she'd meet the guy or guys—Jake did have until the wedding—and see how she got along with him or them. Then she'd think about…more.

The thought made her shudder a little.

She slipped out of the dress she'd just tried on and hung it up—it was a prim flowery number in primary colors. It was too dowdy—too matronly—too…*something*. Anna couldn't put her finger on it. Whatever it was, it just didn't feel right.

"Who did you fix Jake up with?" Emily asked from the other side of the fitting room curtain.

"Her name is Cheryl Woodly. She's a freelance nutritionist who works with new mothers. I met her at the hospital."

"Oh, yeah? What's she like?"

Anna slipped the dress over her head.

"Nice. Smart. Pretty."

"How is she different from Jake's past girlfriends?"

"Did you not hear me say she's *nice* and *smart*? Miss Texas possessed neither of those qualities."

"Me-ow," said Emily.

"I'm only speaking the truth."

"When are they going out?"

"Friday."

Anna stared at herself in the mirror, tugged up on the plunging halter neckline, trying to give *the girls* a little more coverage. She wasn't so sure she wanted to put everything on display on a first date. The dress was great, but it was decidedly not *her*.

"Anna? Did you try on the one I just gave you?"

"Yeah, but—I don't know."

"Come out. Let's see it."

"Nah. Too much cleavage. Too little dress."

Anna hesitated, turning around to check out the back view. She had to admit it was a snappy little number and it looked great from behind. But the front drew way too much focus to the cleavage and that made her squirm.

"Let me see." Before Anna could protest, Emily's face poked through the split in the curtain.

Anna's had flew up to her chest.

"It looks great," Emily said. "The color is out of this world on you. It brings out your eyes. And move your hand."

Emily swatted away her sister's hand from its protective station.

"I don't know what you're afraid of. It accentuates your tiny waist and you're barely showing any cleavage at all. It's just-right sexy. A far cry from those scrubs you hide in every day."

"My scrubs are for work. They're my uniform." Anna turned back to the mirror and put her hands on her hips. She turned to left and then to the right. "You're just jealous that you don't ever get to dress so comfortably at work."

By day, Emily worked in a bank in Dallas and wore suits to work. Because she was saving for a house, two or three times a week she worked as a hostess at Bistro St. Germaine, where she had to dress in sleek, sophisticated black to fit in with the timeless elegance of the downtown Celebration restaurant. Emily had great taste in clothes. Anna would've asked if she could borrow something from her younger sister—and Emily would've graciously dressed her—but it was time for Anna to add a couple of new pieces to her own wardrobe.

"Scrubs are like wearing jammies to work every day," Emily said.

"You know you would if you could," Anna said.

Emily rolled her eyes. "I think you should buy that dress. If not for a date, for you."

"I'll think about it. Now let me change."

Emily stepped back and let Anna close the curtain. Before Anna took off the dress, she did one last three-sixty. It really was cute, in a boho-sexy sort of way.

"Do you really think Jake has some good prospects in mind for you?"

"Who knows? We just talked about this a couple of days ago."

She slipped off the dress and put it with a cute red dress with a bow that tied in front. As she pulled on her jeans and plain white T-shirt, Emily said, "You don't sound very enthusiastic. Are you sure you want to do this?"

"The ball is already rolling. It's just until the wedding. I'll be surprised if it's even five dates. We'll see what happens."

When Anna opened the curtain, she noticed a certain look on her sister's face.

"What?" Anna asked and gathered the clothes, keeping the red and blue dresses separate from the things she didn't want.

"I have to be honest," Emily said. "I always thought you and Jake would end up together."

Her stomach clenched in a way that bothered her more than her sister's words.

"Emily, why would you say that? Jake and I are friends. Good friends. Nothing more."

"Because for better or worse, you two have always stuck together. I mean, I grew up with him, too, but you don't see him hanging out with me. The two of you have always had a really strong bond. Think about it. You and Jake outlasted your marriage. Why the heck are you fixing him up with someone else?"

"Emily, don't. That's not fair."

Anna walked away from her sister.

"Yes, it is. Why is it not fair?"

Anna set the two dresses she wanted to buy on the counter and handed the hanging clothing she didn't want to the sales clerk. After she paid for her purchases and they were outside the Three Sisters shop, Emily resumed the conversation.

"What's not fair about it?"

"You know I can't date Jake. He's my *friend*. He's always been my friend and that's all we will ever be."

Anna felt heat begin to rise up her neck and bloom on her cheeks.

"Then why are you blushing?" Emily asked.

Anna turned and walked to the next storefront, the hardware store, and studied the display as if she'd find the perfect pair of sandals to go with her first-date dress hidden somewhere among the tool kits, ladders and leaf blowers showcased in the window.

Of course, Emily was right behind her. Anna could see her sister's reflection in the glass. She couldn't look at her own as she tried to figure out exactly what was making her so emotional. It wasn't the fact that she was fixing Jake up with someone who could potentially change his mind about marriage being the equivalent of emotional Siberia. Good grief, she was the one who came up with a plan in the first place.

Now Emily's arm was on Anna's shoulder.

"Hey, I'm sorry. I didn't mean to upset you. I'm just a little puzzled by your reaction. I was half teasing, but you're upset. You want to talk about it?"

Anna ran her hand through her hair, feeling a bit perplexed herself.

"I guess it's just the thought of the dating again. You know, starting over. I'm thirty-three years old. This is not where I thought I would be at this age. Em, I want a family. I want a husband who loves me and kids. I never thought I'd be one of those women who felt her biological clock ticking, but mine feels like a time bomb waiting to explode."

The two sisters stood shoulder to shoulder, staring into the hardware store window.

"Well, I guess that eliminates Jake, since we know his thoughts on marriage. Even if he is the hottest guy in town, you don't need to waste your time there."

Anna drew in a deep breath, hoping it would be the antidote to the prickles of irritation that were beginning to feel as if they would turn into full-blown hives.

"Even if he was the marrying kind, he's my best friend, Emily. There are some things you just don't mess with and that's one of them. Hal used to go on and on about how Jake and I secretly wanted each other. Once he even swore there was something going on between Jake and me. But Hal was my husband. I loved him. I loved our marriage and I never cheated. He couldn't get it through his head that a man and a woman could be friends—that there was nothing sexual about it."

"That's probably because in his eyes he couldn't look at a woman without thinking about sex," Emily said. "You know what they say, people usually yell the loudest about the things they're guilty of themselves."

"So, could you just help me out please and not talk about Jake and me in those terms? He's my friend. End of story. Okay?"

Jake had heard a lot of excuses for getting out of a date, and tonight's ranked up there with the best. Cheryl Woodly had called him thirty minutes before he was supposed to pick her up at her place in Dallas for dinner. Her reason for begging off? Her cat, Foxy, had undergone emergency surgery that day and she wasn't comfortable leaving it alone.

He could understand that. He knew people were as crazy about their animals as they were about their children. In some cases, people's animals were their children.

As he turned his 1969 Mustang GTO around and headed back toward Celebration, he realized he wasn't a bit disappointed that Cheryl Woodly had canceled. In fact, from this vantage point, getting out of the blind date seemed like a blessing in disguise. Cheryl had halfheartedly mentioned that maybe they could have a rain check, and he'd made all the right noises and said he'd call her next week to see if they could get something on the books. He wasn't sure if she was preoccupied with her animal or if she was only being polite in suggesting they reschedule. Either way, she didn't seem very enthusiastic. So he wished Foxy the cat well and breathed a sigh of relief.

Still, there was the matter of what to do with the two tickets he'd bought to the Celebration Summer Jazz Festival. He didn't want them to go to waste. Five minutes later, he found himself parking his car in the street in front of Anna's house.

She lived in a Key West–style bungalow two blocks away from downtown Celebration's Main Street. Jake had helped Anna pick out the house after she'd moved to Celebration and her divorce was final.

The place had been a fixer-upper in need of some TLC. Anna had said it was exactly what she wanted—

a project to sink her heart and soul into while she was getting used to her new life. She'd done a great job. Now the house was neat and a little quirky with its fresh island-blue and sea-green paint job. Its style reflected Anna's unique cheerful personality and it always made Jake smile. The lawn was neatly manicured. She must've recently planted some impatiens in the terracotta pots that flanked the porch steps. The flowers' vibrant pinks, fuchsias and reds added another well-planned accent to the already colorful house.

That was the thing about Anna; she put her heart and soul into her home and the place radiated the care she'd invested.

Her Beetle was in the driveway. He could see the inviting faint glow of a light through the living room window.

Good. She was home.

He was going to razz her about her matchmaking skills being a little rusty, since the first date she'd arranged had essentially stood him up. Technically, Cheryl hadn't left him hanging. But Jake was realizing he could get some mileage out of the canceled date and he intended to use it as leverage to get Anna to go to the jazz festival with him tonight.

He'd have a lot more fun with her anyway.

Jake let himself out of the car and walked up the brick path that led to Anna's house. He rapped on the door. *Knock, knock-knock, knock, knock*, their traditional signal that announced they were about to let themselves inside. Really, the knock was just a formality, to keep the other from being surprised. In case she was having sex in the kitchen or something.

Actually, he hadn't been concerned about walking in on Anna having sex because she'd been living like a nun since her divorce. And funny, now that he thought about it, Anna never seemed to come around as much when he was in a relationship.

Hmm. He'd never realized it until right now.

He tried the handle and her door was unlocked. So he let himself in the side door.

"Hey, Anna? It's me."

He heard a muffled exclamation from the other side of the living room. Then Anna stuck her head out of the bedroom door.

"Jake? What are you doing here? Why aren't you out with Cheryl?"

She was hugging the doorjamb and clutching something to her chest as if she were hiding. It looked like she was wearing a dress.

When was the last time he'd seen Anna in a dress?

"She stood me up. What are you all dressed up for? Don't tell me you have a date."

Anna straightened, moving away from the doorjamb, cocking her head to the side.

"She stood you up? Are you kidding me?"

Whoa. She was definitely wearing a dress and she looked *nice.* He'd never realized she had so much going under those scrubs…so much going on *upstairs.* How had he never noticed that before?

The fact made him a little hot and bothered.

He had to force his gaze to stay on her face. Or on her bare feet. Her toenails were painted a sexy shade of metallic blue that matched the dress. Her legs—how had he never noticed her legs before? They were long and lean and tan and looked pretty damn good coming out of the other end of that skirt, which might've been just a hair short…for Anna.

Damn. She sure did look good. No. She looked *hot*.

If she looked like that, why did she cover herself up?

Because this was *Anna*.

He cleared his throat. "Well, she didn't technically stand me up. She called me when I was on my way to get her to say her cat had surgery today and she didn't feel right about leaving it alone."

Anna put her hands on her hips and grimaced. The movement accentuated the low neckline of her dress and the way her full breasts contrasted with her tiny waist that blossomed into hips… Jake forced himself to look away.

"So you didn't shave before you went out? Are you trying to look cool or are you just too lazy?" she asked.

"What?" He rubbed his hand over the stubble on his jaw. "I'm trying to look cool. The ladies like a little five-o'clock shadow."

She quirked a brow and smiled. "Okay, I'll give you that one. It does look pretty…hot."

Something flared inside of him.

"Well, I mean it would be hot if it wasn't *you*."

"What do you mean *if it wasn't me*?"

She shot him a mischievous smile that warmed up her whole face.

"You're messing with me, aren't you?" he said.

"Yeah. I am. It's fun. Oh, I forgot to tell you that Cheryl is a major animal lover. I'm not surprised she wanted to stay home with the cat, but it would've been nice if she could have given you a little more notice."

"Ya think? Where are you going, dressed like that?"

Anna blushed and crossed her arms in front of her, suddenly seeming self-conscious again. It was one of the things he found most endearing about her.

"I'm not going anywhere. I bought some new clothes and I was trying them on so I could figure out what I wanted to wear on my date with Joseph. He texted me today and asked what I was doing next Wednesday. So I figured I needed to decide what I was going to wear. What do you think of this dress? I wasn't so sure, but Emily talked me into getting it."

She put her hands back on her hips and struck a pose. The tags were dangling under her arm and he had an urge to suggest she take it back and exchange it for something a little more modest. Something that didn't make her look like such a knockout.

"It's, uhh… It looks great."

Maybe a little too great for a first date with a guy like Joseph Gardner. He and Joe had been roommates in college while Jake was doing his undergraduate work. Joe lived in Dallas now. He was a friend, a good guy, really. That's why he'd decided to fix him up with Anna.

And that was why his own attitude about the dress confused him.

"In fact, since you're dressed, why don't you give it a test run and wear it to the jazz festival with me tonight?"

Anna groaned and shook her head. "No, Jake, I really wasn't up for doing anything tonight—"

"God, you're so boring." He smiled to let her know

he was just kidding. "Besides, since you fixed me up with a dud, don't you think you owe it to me to not let this extra ticket go to waste?"

She sighed and cocked her head to the side. She smiled at him. He could see her coming around.

"In fact, if we leave now, we will have just enough time to grab something to eat and get over to the pavilion for the first act."

She shook her head. "Jake, I took my makeup off when I got home from work. Can you give me a couple of minutes to fix myself up?"

She looked so good he hadn't even realized she didn't have any makeup on. Her skin was clear and her cheeks and lips looked naturally rosy. Standing there with her auburn hair hanging in loose waves around her shoulders… And with just the right amount of cleavage showing, he couldn't imagine that she could make herself any more beautiful.

Something intense flared inside him. It made him flinch. His instinct was to mentally shake it off. When that didn't work he decided to ignore it, pushing it back into the recesses of his brain where he kept all unwelcome thoughts and memories and other distractions that might trip him up or cause him to feel things that were unpleasant.

It was mind over matter.

Right now, what mattered was him getting his head on straight so that they could get to dinner and the jazz festival.

"You look fine," he said. "Besides, it's just me."

"Yeah, you and the hundreds of other people that will be at the jazz festival. You don't want them looking at you and wondering, Who's that homely woman with Jake Lennox?"

Homely? How could she see herself that way? It didn't make sense.

"Darlin', you are a lot of things, but homely isn't one of them."

She rolled her eyes at him. "Okay. Okay. You don't have to lay it on so thick. Let me get my sandals and we can go."

When she turned around to walk back into the bedroom, his eyes dropped to her backside which swayed gently beneath the fabric of her dress.

What was wrong with him?

Nothing.

Just because Anna was his friend and it had never really registered in his brain that she was an attractive woman, didn't mean she wasn't or that he couldn't appreciate her…from afar.

From very far away. If he knew what was good for him.

But why now?

Why, in the wake of this bet, did it feel as if he was seeing her for the very first time?

Chapter Four

One of the things Anna loved most about Jake was his ability to surprise her. Like tonight, for example. When she'd gotten home from work, she thought she would try on her new dresses, figure out which one she wanted to wear on her date with Joseph, then put on her sweats, make a light dinner and settle in with a good book and a cup of tea.

The last thing she thought she'd be doing was sitting on a red plaid blanket in the middle of downtown Celebration at a jazz festival waving at people she knew, talking to others who stopped by.

But here she was.

And she was enjoying herself.

Who knew?

It was a nice night to be outside. As evening settled

over the town, a nice breeze mellowed the heat of the late June day, leaving the air a luxuriously perfect temperature.

Leave it to Jake to completely turn her plans upside down—and she meant that in the best possible way. He was her constant and her variable. He was her rock and the one who challenged her to leap off the high dive when she didn't even want to leave her house. Like with these dates they were fixing each other up on. The prospect of spending the evening with blind dates felt like a huge leap into the unknown. Without the assurance of a safety net. Yet somehow she knew Jake wouldn't steer her wrong.

She trusted him implicitly.

That's probably why spending the evening with him and his five-o'clock shadow at an event like this—which could actually be quite romantic with the right guy—seemed more appealing than being here with…another guy.

They'd staked out a great place on the lawn in downtown Celebration's Central Park—close enough to the gazebo that they could see the members of the various bands that would be performing tonight, but not so close that they wouldn't be able to talk. Jake had purchased tickets for the VIP area that allowed for the best viewing of the concerts. Leave it to him to do it first-class.

The area was packed with people of all ages: couples, families, groups of friends. All around them, people were talking and laughing and enjoying picnic suppers. There was a happy buzz in the air that was contagious. Suddenly, Anna knew she didn't want to be anywhere else tonight except right here in the middle of this crowd, holding down the fort while Jake went to get them a bottle of wine and their own picnic supper from Celebrations Inc. Catering Company, which had set up a tent at the back of the park.

She'd almost forgotten what it was like to feel like part of a community. Living in San Antonio with Hal had been completely different. Houston was a thriving metropolis; Hal had been kind of a stick-in-the-mud, actually. Picnics and jazz festivals weren't his gig. He was more the type to enjoy eighteen rounds on the golf course, dinner at the club with his stuffy doctor friends and their wives. If the men weren't playing golf, they were talking about it or some scholarly study they'd read about in a medical journal. Anna had tried to join in their conversation once when they were discussing risk factors for major obstetric hemorrhage—after all, she was an OB nurse—but they'd acted as if she'd wanted to discuss the merits of Lucky Charms with and without marshmallows.

Later, Hal had been furious with her. He'd claimed she had embarrassed him and asked her to just do her part and entertain the wives. Never mind that she had zero in common with any of them. She worked, they lunched. She didn't know the difference between Gucci and The Gap—and frankly, she didn't care. Still, she was forced to sit there and listen to them prattle on about who had offended whom on the country-club tennis team and who was the outcast this week because she was sleeping with someone else's husband.

Of course, Anna made the appropriate noises in all

the right places. She'd become an expert at smiling and nodding and sleeping with her eyes open as the women went on and on and on about utter nonsense. Funny thing was, it didn't seem to matter that she had nothing to contribute. They were so busy talking and not listening— too busy formulating what they were going to say next while trying to get a foot in on the conversation—that it didn't even matter that Anna sat there in silence.

Until the last dinner. Anna had sensed the shift in the air even before they sat down to order. The women were unusually interested in *her*. Their eyes glinted as they asked her about her job, the hours she worked. Did she ever work weekends? Nights? How long had she and Hal been married now? How on earth did they make their two-career marriage work?

It reminded her of those days back in elementary school when one kid was chosen to be the student of the week and all the bits and pieces of their lives were put on display for all to see. Of course, the elementary school spotlight was kinder and gentler. The interest was sincere, even if the others really didn't have a burning desire to know.

This sudden interest in her personal life was downright creepy. And she'd left the club that night with the unshakable feeling that something was up. Something was different. They knew something, and like a pride of lionesses, they were going to play with their prey— get maximum enjoyment from the game before the kill.

On the way home Anna had tried to talk to Hal about it, but as usual he wasn't interested.

Exactly one week to the day later—after the niggling feeling that something was *different* grew into a gut-wrenching knowledge that something was very wrong, something that everyone but her seemed to know about—she'd checked Hal's email and everything was spelled out right there. Sexy messages from his office manager. Plans for hookups and out-of-town getaways. The jackass had been so smug in his cozy little affair that he'd left it all right there for her. All she had to do to learn what was really going on was type in his email password, which was the month, day and year of their wedding anniversary.

And Hal had had the nerve to accuse her of being more than just friends—or wanting to be more than just friends—with Jake.

Anna's gaze automatically picked out Jake in the midst of the crowd. As he walked toward her carrying a large white bag in one hand and a bottle of wine in the other, she shoved aside the bad memories of Hal, refusing to let him ruin this night.

She watched Jake as he approached. He was such a good-looking man—tall and broad-shouldered, with dark hair that contrasted with blue-blue eyes. But what mattered even more was that he was a good man, an honest man. He might be a serial monogamist, but he broke up with a woman before he began something with someone else. That was more than she could say for her ex-husband.

It hit her that she was luckier than any of Jake's past girlfriends. They had a connection that went deeper than most lovers. As far as she was concerned, she would do whatever it took to keep their relationship constant.

"They had this incredible-looking bow-tie pasta with rosemary chicken, mushrooms and asparagus," Jake said as he lowered himself onto the blanket. "I got an order of that and they had another type with a red sauce. I picked up a couple of salads and some flatbread. And they had tiramisu. So save room for dessert. Unless you don't want yours. I'll eat it."

"I'll bite your arm if you try to take my dessert."

He held up his hands. "Never let it be said that I came between you and your tiramisu."

"You're a smart man."

Yes, he was.

She took the feast out of the bag and set the containers out on the blanket as Jake opened the red wine and poured it into two plastic cups. He handed one to Anna and raised his, touching the rim to hers.

"Thanks for being such a good sport and coming out here with me tonight," he said. "I would've hated for the tickets to go to waste. Cheryl doesn't know what she's missing."

"Poor Cheryl," Anna said. "No, actually, not poor Cheryl. I understand that she needed to take care of her cat. I wish she could've given you a little more notice."

"No problem," said Jake as he began dishing up pasta on two plates. "I'll probably have a better time with you anyway."

"Are you going to give her another chance?"

Jake gave a noncommittal shoulder roll. "We talked about it, but she didn't sound very eager. If I didn't know better I'd think she changed her mind about the date altogether. But hey, that's fine."

Anna tasted a bite of the bow-tie pasta. It was delicious. She hadn't realized how hungry she was until now, and she had to force herself to chew her food slowly to keep from eating too fast. As she chased down the bite with a swallow of wine, she noticed a couple of women who were sitting in lawn chairs a few feet away from them blatantly looking at Jake and talking to each other. Clearly, they were talking about him.

Really?

She wanted to tell them that they were being obvious.

What if he was on a date tonight? For all they knew, she could've been his girlfriend. They were being so obvious it was rude. Through it all, Jake seemed to be oblivious.

Anna reminded herself that she wasn't his girlfriend. She had no right to feel territorial.

Yeah, what was with that anyway?

She may not have liked Miss Texas—er Dorenda— but she never felt…like *this*.

Then again, she'd always done her best to give Jake and his women plenty of space.

Now that he was free, what was she doing? Why was she meddling? Jake certainly did not want for female attention. And he really wasn't looking to settle down into anything permanent. Maybe Cheryl's canceling was a sign that she needed to back off.

Maybe she should simply enjoy this time with him before he got involved with somebody else—maybe she shouldn't be so quick to pair him up with someone new.

Right. But how was she supposed to get out of the bet now?

* * *

"Is that the blind date you're with?" asked Dylan Tyler, an orthopedic doctor who was brand-new to Celebration Memorial Hospital. He'd come over to say hello after Anna had excused herself to find the ladies' room before the music started.

"No, I'm here with my friend Anna Adams. Do you know her? She is a nurse at the hospital. Works up in OB."

"How did I miss her?" Tyler asked. "You're not going out with her?"

Jake shrugged off Dylan's question.

"If not, introduce me. It's nice to meet new people. I'd certainly like to get to know her better."

I'll bet you would.

Since Tyler had moved to the area, Jake got the feeling the two of them might occasionally *fish in the same pond.* He hoped his colleague wasn't the kind of guy who would poach. Because his interest in Anna encroached a little too close to home.

"I don't think so."

"So you are interested?" Tyler asked. "If so, I'll back off. No problem."

No. He just didn't want someone like Tyler messing with Anna.

Still, Jake nodded.

Dylan Tyler was a good doctor, but he was the last person he'd fix up with Anna. Or one of the last. There were others who were probably worse, but Dylan's overenthusiasm had helped Jake make an instantaneous decision that he wanted to keep the hospital a dating-free zone—for both of them. He'd have to talk to Anna about that as they continued to work out the parameters of this bet they had going on.

Besides, she didn't want to date a doctor anyway. So that automatically ruled out Dr. Dylan Tyler and any lecherous ideas he might have in mind as he tried to get his hands on her.

"No problem, bud. I can take a hint. Anyway, here comes your lady. I'll let you get back to business. You're welcome to join us." With a jerk of his head, Tyler gestured to his party of at least fifteen people, who had set up camp a few yards away from Jake and Anna's blanket for two. "Or if you'd rather be alone, have fun *not dating* her."

Tyler smirked and gave Jake a fist bump before he walked away.

"Who was that?" Anna asked, watching Tyler still watching them—or her. Was the guy blatant or what? She waved at him, obviously wanting to let him know that she was aware of him. It wasn't exactly a flirty move, as much as it was an I-see-you-there act of self-assurance. Even though she had a shy side, when it came to things like this she had a wit that Jake loved.

"That's Dylan Tyler. Orthopedics. He's the new kid in town. Only been at the hospital for about ten days. You haven't met him?"

He knew she hadn't. He just wanted to see what she'd say.

"No. I haven't had the pleasure. He's cute."

Something strange and possessive reared inside Jake. "I thought you said you didn't want to date a doctor."

Anna dragged her gaze from Dylan back to Jake. In the evening light, her blue eyes looked like twin sapphires. "Yes. I did say that, didn't I? Maybe I need to reconsider my criteria. Or at least make an exception. Why let Hal...rob me?"

"What? Rob you of that guy?" Jake asked.

"You look like you smell something gross. Is he that bad?"

Dr. Tyler wasn't really *bad*, but Jake wasn't convinced he was good enough for Anna. Hmm...maybe he identified with Tyler just a little too much? That's why he understood his game.

"Look, you can't keep changing your list of deal breakers," Jake said. "If you do, how am I supposed to know what kind of guy to fix you up with?"

He lowered himself onto the blanket and Anna did, too, gracefully curving her legs around to the side and positioning her dress to cover her thighs. Even so, there was still a whole lot of pretty leg showing.

"Who said anything about not being able to change criteria? The list shouldn't be set in stone, Jake. What if we go out with someone and we realize that something else is a deal breaker, or maybe there's a quality we originally thought was a deal breaker that turns out to not be such a bad thing after all?"

It irritated him the way she glanced in Tyler's direction when she said that.

"If you want me to introduce you to him, I will." He hadn't meant for his voice to hold that much edge.

"Someone's a little touchy tonight." She raised a brow at him.

"I'm just saying, how am I ever going to win this bet if you don't know what you want?" With that, he took care to infuse humor into his tone.

"I don't think either of us knows what we want. If we did, there would be no bet."

Touché.

The first musical group up, a Rastafarian reggae-jazz fusion band, took the stage and preempted their conversation. After a short warm-up, they got the party started with a Bob Marley tune, which got most of the crowd to its feet. Some people swayed, while others sang along.

After the first song ended, the singer in his smooth Jamaican accent shouted, "Hello, all of you beautiful people. We are so happy to be here tonight. How are you all feeling?"

As the crowd cheered, Jake and Anna exchanged glances that seemed to call a truce to the discussion they'd had a moment ago.

"We are releasing our first CD next month and we would like to introduce you to the first single from that album. It's all about feeling the love and sharing it. Isn't that a great thought? Wouldn't you like to fill the world with love?"

As the band broke into the first strains of their song, the singer said, "I want to see everybody on their feet. Let's all dance and sing and fill the world with love. I don't want to see anybody sitting down looking sad."

Jake took her Anna's hand and pulled her to her feet.

"Oh, no, you're not—"

"Oh, yes I am."

He pulled her in close, holding one of her hands

down at their sides as she placed her other hand on his shoulder and he placed his hand on the small of her back and sent her out for a twirl. Back in middle school, they had learned to swing dance in PE. It was something that the two of them still loved to do, though he couldn't remember the last time they had gone dancing. Anna's husband, Hal, hadn't been very understanding. So Jake had let it go so as not to rock the boat.

Other than their Sadness Intervention Dance, it had been far too long since they'd done that. They weren't the only ones dancing; it seemed a good part of the crowd had been inspired by the Rastafarian singer as he sang his song of spreading joy and love.

It was funny how even after all these years the steps moved through him and into Anna and back to him, the steps and twirls pulling each other together and breaking them apart, but ultimately reeling them back in.

Maybe it was the wine or the music, or it could have even been the setting sun that was sinking lower in the evening sky and bathing everything in a warm golden glow, but for the first time in a long time Jake felt as if he didn't have a care in the world.

As the song wound down, the Rastafarian hopped down off the bandstand into the audience and was encouraging people to fall in love, "at least for tonight. Love the one you're with and send a message of love and good energy out into the world."

Jake gave Anna one final flourishing spin and reeled her back in so that they stood face-to-face, still in each other's arms. Jake's hands moved slowly up her back and over her shoulders until his fingers cupped her face.

His body knew what he was going to do before his mind could stop him.

He bent his head and covered her lips with his.

She didn't pull away. She accepted the kiss like a gift. A gift that was as much for him as it was her.

Her mouth was soft and yielding.

She sighed, a feminine little shudder of a breath, and he pulled back the slightest bit to allow her to object.

But she didn't.

So, he took that to mean that she had accepted his gift and leaned in and kissed her with hunger, and conviction and a need that made the axis of his world shift.

And she kissed him back.

He didn't care that they were in the middle of downtown Celebration in Central Park where anyone could see. Hell, for all he knew, her parents and sister or his brothers might be watching him kiss his best friend, Anna Adams. But he didn't care. Because, for that moment, they were the only two people in the world.

It was just him wanting her and her kissing him back.

Chapter Five

Jake wasn't avoiding Anna.

But he wasn't at all positive she wasn't avoiding him.

He had no idea what had gotten into him Friday night. One minute they'd been dancing and having a great time, and then they were kissing. He wasn't sure who had started it—or if it even mattered. The thing was, he'd kissed his best friend, and at the time neither of them seemed to mind. In fact, it felt good…as if it worked.

Would they work? The two of them…?

It should've felt like kissing his sister. But it hadn't. It felt warm and ripe and *right*. At least in the moment. Then they had done a damn good job of settling down and pretending as if nothing had happened. They'd watched the rest of the concert with a respectable amount of space between them on the blanket. He'd taken her home, walked her to the door and they'd wished each other a platonic good-night.

To the untrained eye, it might've looked as if nothing had happened between them. But then they'd gone all weekend without talking to each other. Proof positive that all was not well and it simply shouldn't have happened.

Jake couldn't remember the last time he and Anna had gone two days without talking. Not since she'd moved back to Celebration. Even when he'd been dating Dorenda and the women who had come before her, he and Anna had talked. They may not have seen each other every day, but they'd talked. Now everything felt off balance and he knew it would stay that way until one of them broke the ice. And that was exactly what he intended to do.

It was eleven-thirty on Monday morning and he'd be damned if he was going to let this weirdness go on a moment longer. He did his best to isolate the kiss, to box up the memory of it and relegate it to the places in his mind where he kept things he didn't want to think about, the things that got in the way.

With that done, he realized that on a normal day by now, he probably would have already seen her—razzed her about whether or not she'd seen Dr. Dylan Tyler today and probably asked her if she had plans for lunch.

He might've been a little behind schedule, but it wasn't too late to man up and get up to speed.

The elevator opened on the maternity ward on the third floor of the hospital. It wasn't his usual territory.

He generally stayed one floor below on the second floor. But every so often—mostly when he wanted to see Anna—he'd find his way up here.

It must've been a slow morning, because three nurses stood talking behind the main desk. They looked up and one blushed as he approached.

"Hi, Dr. Lennox," said one nurse. Her name was Marissa. He knew that because Anna always spoke highly of her. "How can I help you?"

Jake glanced down the empty hallway toward the patient rooms, but didn't see any sign of his friend. The sound of a newborn crying cut through the air.

"Hi, Marissa, ladies. Is Anna around?"

On the wall behind the desk a bulletin board was full to overflowing with baby and family pictures, thank-you notes and pictures drawn in crayon. A call light came on, signaling that a patient needed help and one of the nurses—he wasn't sure of her name and she wasn't wearing a name tag—excused herself to tend to the woman.

"No, we're pretty slow up here today. But I hear you're hopping downstairs. The chief asked if Anna would come down there and help until y'all are caught up. I'm surprised you didn't see her since that's your floor."

"Really? How long had she been there?"

The two nurses exchanged a glance. "Probably since about ten o'clock," said the one whose name tag read "Patty."

So Anna had been on his floor for an hour and a

half and she hadn't said anything. Okay, this definitely called for an intervention.

"I guess that just shows you how busy we've been," said Jake. "Thanks, ladies."

As he turned to walk away, Patty said, "Did you have fun at the jazz festival Friday night? I saw you there and I wanted to get over to say hello, but…" Patty and Marissa exchanged another look. "You saw for yourself how crowded it was and, well, I didn't want to interrupt. Y'all looked like you were having such a good time."

Patty's words were like a well-landed kick in the gut.

Great. Just great. All they needed was to become a rumor on the hospital grapevine. He should've thought of that before losing his mind Friday night.

He stared at the women for a moment, unsure of what to say. After all, what did one say to a comment so full of insinuation?

It's none of your business?

Quit gossiping?

Get back to work?

What an inappropriate thing for them to say. Celebration Memorial didn't have an uptight work atmosphere, but they still adhered to a certain level of professionalism.

They must've read his irritation on his face, because their smiles gradually faded. He hoped they hadn't been this out of line with Anna. But if Patty felt free enough to be that bold with him, he had a sinking feeling he'd better find Anna fast and make sure everything was okay.

"Ladies." He gave them a curt nod and turned back toward the elevator.

This was case in point of why it was a bad idea to date anybody he worked with. He was sure Anna would tell him the same thing once they had a chance to talk.

Relationships were complicated enough. Things like this made them worse. There may have been one day of gossip when he and Dorenda broke up, but it had faded and everyone went on about their business.

Honestly, he hadn't cared what everyone was saying. But this was different.

Now every time he and Anna were together, people would be speculating. He didn't worry for himself; he worried about how it would make Anna feel.

The elevator dinged and Jake steeled himself to see someone else who might've been at the festival, someone who would give him a sidelong, raised-eyebrow look. But when the door slid open, a man holding a little girl in one arm and a giant vase of roses in another smiled at him as he stepped out into the hall. Jake smiled back and let them clear out before he got in and pressed the button for the second floor.

To hell with them. To hell with them all. Except Anna.

If he could have a do-over, Friday night would be it. Never in his life had he wanted to take back something so badly. Well, of course the other big do-over would be to go back and make things right with his mother. All those years that she'd lived with that secret and let her sons believe she was the culprit who caused the splintering of their family, when in actuality their dad had given her a very good reason to leave. And he'd been content to take the secret to his grave.

If Jake's indiscretion with Anna was his reason for not dating coworkers, his mom and dad's story was the case against marriage. Marriage could turn everything you believed in into a lie. You thought you knew someone, and it turned out they were a complete stranger. Then you had to wreck a lot of lives to get back to the truth.

Jake scrubbed his eyes with his palm, trying to scour away the regret. He had too much to do today to worry about things he couldn't change.

When he stepped out of the elevator on the second floor, Anna was at the nurses' station. She looked up and their gazes snagged. For a split second, she looked like a deer caught in headlights, but then the warm smile that he loved so much spread across her face and he knew everything was going to be okay.

"There you are," he said as he walked toward the nurses' station.

"Here I am," she said. "I didn't know I was lost."

"Actually, I'm probably the one who is lost. I had no idea you were working down here today. I just went up to three to find you."

Her smile froze and her eyes got large and she didn't have to say a word for him to know that Patty and Marissa had probably given her a more intense grilling than they had given him.

He wondered what she'd said, but this was not the time or the place to ask her.

He looked at his watch. "Hey, I was wondering if you wanted to grab a bite of lunch."

Anna's face fell. "I just got back from lunch. I only

took a half hour since we're so busy. I wish I'd known—I would've waited."

"Hey, no problem—"

"Excuse me, Dr. Lennox," said Cassie Davis, one of the surgical floor nurses. "The family of Mr. Garrity, who is in room 236, is here and they have some questions for you. I told them you probably wouldn't be able to meet with them right now, but I said I would ask. But if you're just getting ready to go to lunch, I can tell them you're busy."

Jake shook his head. "No, I can talk to them now. It's fine."

Cassie handed Jake the patient's chart. "Thank you," he said to her as she walked to the opposite side of the nurses' station. When she was out of earshot, he said to Anna, "Let's talk later. Okay?"

She nodded.

"Maybe tonight?" he said. "Do you want to grab a bite after work?"

Anna closed the computer file she had been working on. "Actually, I can't. I have a date. Over the weekend, Joseph Gardner, the guy you set me up with, texted and asked if we could move our date from Wednesday to tonight. We're going ice-skating."

Ice-skating in June? That was different. Good. It meant she would have to cover up. She'd have to wear something like jeans and a turtleneck. Multiple layers on top. Maybe even a scarf around her neck.

Anna gave a little shrug. She looked unimpressed.

"Oh, okay. Have fun."

All Jake could think was, thank God she wouldn't be wearing that blue-and-white dress.

Have fun?
Oh, okay. Thanks.
Was that all he had to say?
Then again, what did she want him to say?
"Dr. Lennox is such a great guy," said Cassie. There was a dreamy note in her voice. "Why can't all doctors in this hospital be more like him?"

Anna followed Cassie's gaze and saw her watching Jake disappear into Mr. Garrity's room.

"Nice and so good-looking…" Cassie sighed, looking absolutely smitten. "A rare combination in these halls, wouldn't you say?"

"You've got that right."

Actually, truer words had never been spoken. Anna knew all about good-looking doctors who were not of the nice variety. Her husband, Hal, had been smart and handsome, but sometimes he could be the most insensitive, obtuse SOB you could have ever imagined. When he was irritated or bored, he let his feelings hang out there. He could be caustic and rude.

If he'd been on his way to lunch, the patient's family would've had to wait. His philosophy was, if you didn't set boundaries, coworkers and patients and their families wouldn't set them for you.

On paper, his argument was valid. The only problem was, he didn't seem to realize that other people had boundaries and feelings…and needs.

Jake always seemed to have a moment for anyone who asked, yet he never acted as if he felt compromised.

Anna hoped Friday night hadn't compromised their friendship.

There was no denying that the kiss had blown her mind. She'd never really given much thought to what it would be like to kiss Jake, but now she couldn't get it out of her mind.

All weekend long she'd felt his hands on her body, felt the phantom sensation of his lips moving on hers. He tasted wonderful, like red wine and chocolate-laced espresso from the tiramisu. Flavors that were rich and dark and delicious. Flavors that a girl might start craving once she got a taste.

And she couldn't even believe she was linking cravings and Jake Lennox in the same thought.

What's wrong with me? Am I in high school?

No, because in high school Jake had always been like a brother she'd never had.

Now she'd gone and kissed him. And he wanted to talk.

Talk. That couldn't be good. He hadn't kissed her at the door Friday night—would she have wanted him to? That needy, greedy part of her that could still taste him probably wouldn't have objected if he had. But the logical, sensible Anna knew they were flirting with disaster.

She knew what he was going to say. That the kiss had been a mistake. That they needed to pretend it never happened.

She bit her bottom lip.

They didn't need to discuss it. As far she was concerned it was forgotten.

Ha, ha! Now they'd satisfied that little curiosity, it was time to put it behind them.

She felt her phone vibrate in the pocket of her scrubs, signaling a text. She pulled it out and looked at it. It was from Joseph Gardner, her date tonight.

Maybe he was canceling. *God, wouldn't that be great.*

But then she saw the message he left.

Looking forward to ice-skating tonight and seeing if we might fall for each other.

What?

She cringed. Oh, God, that was a bad pun. Ice-skating and falling.

No. Just no.

"Everything okay?" Cassie asked.

Anna hadn't realized Cassie had walked up behind her. The woman seemed to be the only one in the hospital who hadn't heard about her public display of... friendship with Jake.

"Yes. Fine."

She dropped her phone back into her pocket as if it was a hot potato and took a deep breath.

With her attitude, she probably had no business going out with this poor guy. Really, the text was sweet. Corny, but sweet. Despite the fact that she hadn't even met him in person, it showed that he had a sense of humor. It was the kind of gesture that a woman would find very endearing if she was into the man who'd sent it.

But for the woman who wasn't even looking forward to the date…

Stop it, Anna. What kind of horrible attitude is that?

Joseph Gardner had taken time out of his day to text her. She should consider it a good sign. She should be nice.

Or maybe she should save him the brunt of her bad humor and cancel…

She drummed her fingernails on the desk for a moment, contemplating what to do. Then she pulled her phone out of her pocket again and texted Joseph back.

Anna had insisted on meeting Joseph Gardner at the ice rink in Celebration. Even if this guy was a friend of Jake's and an established investment banker, she didn't know him. Besides, she liked the idea of having an escape in case she wanted to leave.

She arrived at the skating rink right on time, with her socks and her gloves and the determination to come into this evening with a better attitude than she had had today.

She wouldn't think of Jake and his lips and his taste of red wine and chocolate.

Nope. She wasn't gonna invite him along on this date.

She got out of the car and walked up to the window where they sold admission. She looked around, but she didn't see anyone who might remotely be Joseph.

Should she wait for him out here? Or should she go inside and get her skates?

But if she went inside, that meant she would pay for

herself. She had no problem with that; in fact part of her preferred it because then there would be no feelings of anybody owing anyone anything.

But it was awkward. Should she buy his ticket, too? No. That would be weird.

At heart, she was a traditionalist who enjoyed being treated like a lady. But it didn't necessarily mean she wasn't a lady if she paid her own way.

She really was so bad at this.

No. Not bad. Just a little rusty.

And he was late.

Anna got in line. The box office was manned by a lone teenage boy who didn't seem to be in a hurry for anything. It took about five minutes to get to the window.

"One admission, please, for the seven o'clock skating session. I'll need to pay for skate rental, too."

The teenager checked his phone and answered a text before he methodically punched numbers into the cash register. No wonder it was taking so long. But why should she be in a hurry?

"That'll be ten bucks. Four for the skates, six for admission."

As she was fishing her wallet out of her purse, she wondered if she should wait a few minutes longer. What if he didn't show? Did she really want to be stuck here all evening?

It's not like I have to stay if he doesn't show.

As she opened her wallet, someone behind her said, "Anna? Are you Anna Adams?"

She turned around and saw a tall, thin, blond man with sparkling brown eyes.

"Joseph?"

"The one and only. I'm sorry I'm late. You know, when longshoremen show up late for work they get docked."

She blinked at him. She might've even frowned because she had no idea what he was talking about.

"Longshoremen," he repeated. "They get *docked.* It's a joke."

"Oh!" Anna forced a laugh, even though it really wasn't funny. It was kind of sophomoric, actually. But she wanted to be a good sport. "I get it. You're a *punny* guy, aren't you, Joseph?"

His eyes lit up and he opened his mouth and pointed at her. "That was good. I think I'm going to like you. Put your money away. When I ask a woman out, I pay. So this is on me."

She held her breath, waiting for him to deliver another pun, but he didn't. So she stuffed the ten-dollar bill back into her wallet.

"Thank you, Joseph. Do you go by Joseph? Or should I call you Joe?"

He took their tickets and stepped away from the window, motioning toward the door. "Yeah, it's Joseph. And you can call me Joseph."

Umm? Oh. "Okay. Joseph."

"No, actually you can call me Joe. I'm just kidding you."

Was that supposed to be funny?

They waited while a family of four entered the building. Then Joseph held the door for Anna, allowing her to step inside first.

At least he was a gentleman.

Inside, the place was at least thirty degrees cooler than it had been outside; the smell of freshly popped popcorn and hot dogs mingled with the scent of dampness. The sound of video games warred with loud music. The rink was already buzzing with activity, but an uncomfortable silence had wedged itself between Anna and Joe. As they waited in line to get their ice skates, Anna could feel the nervous energy radiating off her date. She sort of felt bad for the guy.

She'd been anxious about meeting him, but now she wanted to take him by the shoulders, look him in the eyes and tell him to take a deep breath. He didn't have to try so hard.

Maybe *she* needed to try a little harder to take a little of the pressure off him.

"What do you do, Joe?"

"I'm an investment banker, but I'm starting to lose interest."

He laughed, then cleared his throat when he noticed that Anna was grimacing.

"So you're a nurse?" he said. "Did you hear about the guy whose entire left side was cut off? He's all *right* now."

Anna winced.

"You better slow down there, buddy. You don't want a use up your best material before they Zamboni the ice for the first time."

He looked a little embarrassed. "Too much, huh?"

Anna held up her thumb and index finger so that they were about an inch apart. "Just a tad."

She didn't want to be mean, but really, was there anything much worse than canned humor? Couldn't he hear himself? A horrifying thought crossed her mind—that he could hear himself, but just couldn't *help* this incessant need to make a joke out of everything.

Was there a name for that sort of disorder? Or was it a defense mechanism?

Either way, at this rate, it was going to be a long night. She sat down on the bench to put on her skates. She'd have to ask Jake if his pal Joe had been the class clown.

In all fairness, she'd told Jake that humor was high on her list. She loved to laugh. Who didn't? But no one liked to be pelted with nonstop rehearsed repertoire.

By the grace of God, Joe managed to contain himself as they finished putting on their skates.

After she put on her gloves, Anna stood, wobbling a little bit. Joe reached out a hand, which she grabbed to steady herself.

"It's been a long time since I've been ice-skating. Hope I can still do it."

She braced herself for another pun, vaguely fearing that she'd left herself wide-open by saying that, but either Joe was out of material or he was showing some restraint.

"Jake told me you were athletic. That's why I thought this would be fun."

Fun. Okay, that was a good sign. If he could stop

with the bad jokes, she could loosen up a little bit and have fun.

They made their way into the rink. He stepped onto the ice first, looking sure of himself and steady. He held out his hand and helped Anna. She wobbled again, but managed to grab the bar attached to the shoulder-high wall surrounding the ice. But soon enough, she found her balance and they began circling the rink. He seemed to understand Anna's need to hug the wall for the first couple of rounds. For the most part, he stayed next to her, but showed off a little bit, skating backward every now and then.

At least he didn't try to hold her hand.

Was it natural for a man in his thirties to be this good at ice-skating?

She gave herself a mental slap for being so judgmental.

When the music changed to a slow song and the DJ dimmed the light and turned on the disco ball, Joe turned around to skate backward and started to reach for her.

"I need a break," Anna said. "How about we sit this one out?"

They made their way to a table in the concession area. Joe got them hot chocolate and a tub of popcorn. Anna had to give him props for getting it to the table without dropping, sloshing or spilling. She wouldn't have been so adroit.

He set the drinks on the table and they sat quietly as they watched the skaters float by in pairs.

"Do you have any hobbies? Or do you play any sports?"

"I like basketball."

It made sense. He was tall and moved well. So, okay. Good. Now they were getting somewhere.

"When I'm playing, I always wonder why the basketball keeps getting bigger, and then it hit me."

She blinked at him. The guy just couldn't stop. She was going to kill Jake. Why in the world would he fix her up with an amateur comedian?

"So I imagine that right about now, you want to throw something at me, don't you?" he said.

Yes.

She smiled and shrugged.

"If you do, I hope you'll make it a soda—"

"Because it's a soft drink," Anna finished. She shook her head.

Okay. That's enough. There was being a good sport and then there was being a martyr. Was this the kind of guy Jake saw her with? Just what part of this did he think she would find attractive? No offense to Joe. He was a good guy and would make the right woman happy—hysterically happy. But he wasn't for her. Clearly, her heart was somewhere else.

"So, Jake told me you're divorced," Joe said. Even though this was a topic Anna generally wouldn't want to talk about with a stranger, and certainly not on a first date, it was Joe's first real attempt to make conversation that wasn't a setup for a pun.

"I am. The divorce was official a month ago, but we've been broken up for about two years now."

Joe stared at his hands for a moment.

When he looked up, Anna saw something that re-sembled vulnerability in his eyes.

"It's only been six months for me," he said. "Does it get easier?"

So that explained it—his nervousness, his need to cover up by making dumb jokes. Well, maybe that was just part of his personality. But she felt bad for the guy. He was obviously hurting.

"It does. It just takes time. If it makes you feel any better, you are my first date since my divorce."

And Jake was your first kiss.

Knock it off, Anna. Stay in the moment.

Joe's eyes lit up the way they did when he was about to bomb her with a bad joke. Anna held up her hand and he stopped.

"Joe, you're a nice guy, and I can't deny that you are just as rusty at this as I am. But the jokes and the puns… maybe use them like salt and pepper?"

He looked sheepish.

"I don't mean to be a bitch. Really, I don't. Can you just think of it as—?"

She started to say *tough love*, but she didn't want to give him the wrong idea.

"Think of it as a friend being brutally honest."

Had Jake planned on dishing out a heaping helping of brutal honesty when he'd asked her to lunch today?

"You're right," he said. "I appreciate your brutal hon-esty. I guess it might be a little too soon for me to be getting out there again. Obviously."

"You'll be a fun date when you are finally ready,"

said Anna. She wanted to add, *when you meet the right woman*, but she was sure he already knew that.

The couples' skate ended, the lights were restored to their earlier brightness and a faster, decidedly less romantic tune sounded from the speakers.

"Shall we head back out there?" he asked.

She stood. "I need to go to the ladies' room. How about if I meet you on the ice?"

As she scooted out of the booth, Joe stood—just like a gentleman should. But somewhere between scooting and standing, the toe of her skate connected with something hard and the next thing Anna knew she was pitching forward, sticking her hands out to keep from doing a face-plant.

Her wrists bore the brunt of her fall. As Joe pulled her to her feet, a white-hot pain shot down the fingers of her left hand and up to her elbow. She pulled her hand into her chest, cradling it, but trying to not draw any more attention to herself than she already had.

She must've been a lousy actress.

"Are you okay?" Joe asked, reaching for her hand. "Let me look at that. You didn't break it, did you?"

She could move her fingers, but the movement sent flashes of pain spiraling through her.

"I don't think it's broken, but it hurts."

"Let me get you some ice," he offered. "This place should have plenty."

He was almost to the concession stand before she could object. Then, by the time he returned, she knew the night was over.

"Thank you for the ice, Joe. But I think I should go. I'm sorry."

"Should we go to the hospital and get it x-rayed?" he said. "I'll go with you. I hate it that you got hurt."

"No, thank you for offering, though. I'm a nurse. I'm sure it's not fractured. It's probably just a sprain. But I think I should go and ice it down and take care of it. The last thing I need is to fall on it again. Given my graceful performance tonight, that's not so far-fetched."

Joe looked a little relieved. "Aren't we a pair? You with your sprained wrist and me with my bad jokes."

He didn't have to say any more for Anna to know that he wasn't really feeling the chemistry either. Despite everything, it made the night better. Sort of like negatives canceling each other out to make a positive.

"Let me drive you home, at least," he said. "I'll arrange to get your car tomorrow."

"No. But thank you, Joe. I don't live too far from here. Really, I'll be fine. Thank you for everything."

As she extended her good hand to shake his, she looked into his earnest brown eyes. There was a woman out there who would love Joseph Gardner's quirky sense of humor. He truly was a good guy. Sadly, he just wasn't the guy for her.

Chapter Six

"What did you do to your hand?" Jake wasn't calling Anna to check up on the date. In fact, he hadn't planned on calling her at all that night, but what kind of friend wouldn't have checked on her after learning she'd fallen at the ice-skating rink and had hurt herself?

"Jake? I'm fine. How did you know?"

He explained that Joe had called him and given him the scoop.

"What else is there to tell you?" Anna asked.

"Why don't you let me have a look at your hand?"

He knew what her reaction would be, and that's why he'd driven over before she could tell him not to.

"Jake, you didn't have to drive all the way over here. I'm sore, but I really don't think it's broken."

He got out of the car and started walking up the brick path.

"I was in the neighborhood."

"You and I do not live in the same neighborhood."

"Well, I'm here now. In fact, I'm standing outside your front door. Are you going to let me in or not?"

"Sure."

He would've let himself in like he always had, but now… Now that Anna was dating, he thought it would be best to respect her privacy. Although part of him was a little surprised when she did not comment on the fact that he'd knocked when he'd always let himself in in the past.

He glanced at his watch. It was nearly nine o'clock. She'd probably already locked up for the night. In fact, if she hadn't, he was going to say something. Insist that she be more careful. Celebration was as close to being a crime-free community as one could hope for, but she was a single woman living alone. Just to make sure she wasn't compromising herself, Jake reached out and tried the door.

It was locked. As it should be. *Good.*

The porch light flicked on, followed by the sound of the dead bolt turning and the big wooden door opening. His heart clenched when he saw her standing there with her left arm in a makeshift sling. She was wearing a soft-looking pink T-shirt with blue pajama bottoms patterned with white sheep—or they might have been cumulus clouds. He didn't want to look too closely; besides he was more concerned with the drawn look on her face and the dullness in her eyes that indicated that she was in considerable pain.

"What did you do to yourself?"

She stepped back and let him inside, closing the door behind them.

"I don't know why I thought I could escape tonight unscathed," she said as he followed her into the family room off the kitchen. There was a pregnant pause and for a moment he wasn't sure if she was talking about the date or the ice-skating. He decided to wait for her to continue rather than ask.

"I guess I'm not as young as I thought I was."

"Don't be ridiculous. You are one of the most athletic people I know."

"Obviously, I'm no Tara Lipinski."

She sat down on the couch and gestured for him to take a seat next to her.

"No medals?"

"Only if they gave awards for klutziness—I'd win the gold. I wasn't even on the ice when I fell. If I was going to walk away with battle wounds, at least I could've had a good story to tell—that I landed wrong when I attempted my triple Salchow sequence. But no, I tripped over the leg of the table in the snack bar. There's a story for my grandkids."

Jake knew it was only a figure of speech, but Anna did see grandkids in her future. She wanted them—like most normal, healthy women. And she should have a family—a husband who loved her, a house full of kids and even more grandkids.

He could never give her that.

Not that she was thinking about him that way, he hoped. Everything had just gotten so muddied since the kiss. At least it had for him.

"Let me take a look at that." He reached out and eased the scarf that she was using as a makeshift sling over her head. She smelled good. Like shampoo and that flowery perfume she wore. The closeness and the smell of her and the act of lifting the scarf off her body conjured visions of him leaning in and kissing her again and taking off her shirt—

What the hell was wrong with him?

He was here to help her, not mentally undress her.

Holding her injured hand, he moved his knee away from hers to put a little distance between them. He tried to ground himself firmly in the reality that he was holding her hand because he was a doctor. And she was in pain, for God's sake. Never mind that her fingers were long and slender and her wrist was fine-boned, despite the swelling. He could tell that when he compared it to the one that wasn't injured.

He'd known her all these years, yet he'd never noticed this? How had that happened?

"Can you move your fingers?"

"I can." She demonstrated slowly, but grimaced from the pain.

"How about your wrist?"

"Yep." She lifted her hand from his and circled it in the air. "Ouch."

She lowered her hand back into his, palm side up, and he lightly stroked her skin with his thumb. She was so soft, so—

"I know this hurts," he said. "I'm sorry. But just one more test. Can you make a fist?"

"I can, but I don't want to because it hurts."

"I think we should take you in and get an X-ray," Jake said. "Just as a precaution."

He was still cradling her hand in his. Now he was using his other hand to lightly caress the soft skin on her inner forearm.

"Would you let me take you to the hospital?"

She pulled her hand from his, holding it against her chest.

"No, Jake." She looked almost panicked.

"Why not?"

"Because if we come into the ER together at this time of night, it's just going to perpetuate the rumors."

Oh. God, that's right.

He raked his hand through his hair. "You know what? I don't give a damn what they think. I don't care what they're saying. We are none of their business."

We?

They weren't a *we.* Well, they were, but not *that kind* of *we.*

Anna sat back on the couch. "Yeah, that's easy for you to say because you don't have to hear what they're saying. Since you're a doctor, they talk about you, but not to you."

He frowned. "Oh, I heard about it all right, from Patty who works with you up in OB."

Okay, so she had a point about the gossip. Yes, if they came in together tonight, the rumors would be flying tomorrow.

"But, Anna, if you need an X-ray, you need an X-ray. As your attending physician, I am suggesting that you get this looked at just to be sure."

"You are not my doctor. You're my—" She shook her head. "You're my friend." She held up her hand. "If it were broken, I couldn't do this." She made a fist with her hand and shook it at him, but no sooner had she done it than she gasped from the pain.

Now he was shaking his head.

"You need an X-ray."

"Not tonight."

"You have to be one of the most stubborn women I've ever met."

She shrugged. "Well, the least you could do is go get me some ice. Even Joe was nice enough to do that. Before you called, I was using that bag of frozen peas." She nodded in the direction of a bag lying atop a magazine on the coffee table. "But I think it's spent. I could probably use a full-fledged ice pack. There's a box of zipper baggies in that drawer in the kitchen. You know where the ice is."

He gave her a look, but he spared her the lecture about refusing physicians' orders. She was right—he wasn't her doctor. And she was a smart woman. She knew her body. Then again, sometimes health-care workers were the worst when it came to taking care of themselves in situations like this.

"Jake. The ice? Please?" Then as if she were reading his mind she added, "If the pain gets any worse, I'll have it x-rayed when I get to work tomorrow."

He came back with the ice and handed it to her.

"Do you want me to go to the pharmacy and get you something for the pain?"

"No, thanks. You know I'm no good on strong meds. I took some ibuprofen when I got home. It's starting to take the edge off."

"Speaking of, how did you get along with Joe?"

He knew she might not be in the mood to talk about it, but it didn't hurt to ask. He was curious, and Joe had been a little tight-lipped on the phone, not really sharing much other than the fact that Anna had fallen and wouldn't let him take her to the hospital.

"He's a nice guy deep down. But did you really think he was my type? He kept cracking these really corny jokes. I mean it was rapid-fire, one right after the other. Did he act like that when you roomed with him in college?"

Had he?

"I guess he was a little annoying, but that was a while ago. Because if I were he, I would've grown up a little by now."

"I think he uses humor to deflect his pain. He hasn't been divorced for that long."

"I guess not. Maybe he's not over his ex. Maybe it was too soon."

"Why would you fix me up with someone who'd recently gone through a divorce?"

Jake rolled his shoulders. What was he supposed to say? *Because the two of you had that in common.* Obviously, he was not a matchmaker. Obviously, he didn't have a clue.

"Not your type, huh?"

"No." He wasn't sure if she was annoyed or if it was the pain bleeding through into her words.

His gaze fell to her bottom lip. He was irrationally relieved that Joe hadn't kissed her. He couldn't quite reconcile that feeling. He knew she was off-limits to him. He'd fixed her up with Joe, thinking they might get along. Or if he thought about it a little more, he realized that she and Joe probably had nothing in common.

"Good to know," he said. "Maybe it's not a bad idea to have a debriefing after each of the dates so that we can figure out what worked and what didn't work, so that the next time, we come closer to getting it right. What do you think?"

"If you'll actually go on the next date I set up for you, you might not need next time."

He had the strongest urge to ask her if she wanted to talk about what happened between them at the jazz festival. He realized it was completely out of context, but here she was still hell-bent on introducing him to the perfect woman.

A voice way back in the recesses of his brain challenged him to consider the possibility that the perfect woman was sitting right here in front of him.

But no. Oh, no. *Hell, no.* He wasn't about to go there. He couldn't.

He lowered himself onto the couch next to her face-forward so he wouldn't have to look at her.

"So, using Joe as a point of reference, what should I do differently when I arrange the next date?"

She thought about it for a moment. She laid her head back on the couch and stared at the ceiling.

"Well, I liked the fact that Joe acted like a gentleman. He got points in that area, but there was zero attraction."

Good.

"And of course there's funny, and then there's annoying. In that area, Joe bordered on annoying. So, next time maybe go with somebody perhaps a bit more intelligent, someone kind and someone who hasn't just come from signing divorce papers."

She sat up and rearranged the ice pack on her wrist inside the sling, then looked at him.

"I have an idea," she said. "One thing that might be making this difficult is that we've never seen each other in action out on a date."

"You saw me with Dorenda."

"I felt like I needed to avert my eyes when you and Dorenda were together. Either that, or tell you to get a room. The PDA was really unbearable."

"So what are you getting at?" he asked.

"For our next date, why don't we go on a double date? That way we can see each other in action. Of course, it will have to wait until I'm feeling better. But let's start looking at prospects."

"All right," he said. "That could be interesting. But I'm still unclear about something you said. Did you say you didn't want to date anyone who is divorced?"

"No, that's not what I meant. I understand that when you get into your thirties, most guys are going to come with some baggage. We're not spring chickens anymore. So, yes, divorced is okay—I'd be a bit hypocritical if I ruled out all divorced men. Actually, what scares me more at this point in the game is the ones who have never been married. There're usually issues with them, too."

He nudged her with his knee. "Need I remind you that I've never been married? I don't have issues."

"I hate to break it to you, but you have more issues than most guys."

He made a face as if he was offended. "I don't have issues. I just know what I want."

"You never want to get married."

They sat in silence for a moment, her words ringing in the air.

Finally, she turned to him. "Jake, I know your mom left your family and it was hard on you boys. I saw what you went through. I lived it with you. Even as bad as it was, you, your brothers and your dad were always close. I really don't understand how you can let her leaving your family rob you of one of the most wonderful experiences of life. It's made you so dead-set against getting married. Most women out there aren't going to be like your mother. They'll be faithful and loving wives. A wife is someone you can count on. It goes beyond the sex and having kids. A husband and wife are a team. Your spouse is someone you can count on when nobody else in the world has your back. Forgive me for saying this, because I know your mom is gone, but she was wrong. She took the easy way out. And you shouldn't have to keep suffering for her bad decision."

The day his mom left the family, she'd tried to take the kids with her, but of course his dad had put up a fight. His dad had told her, "It may be your choice to divorce yourself from this family, but I'll be damned if you're going to take my boys."

Two days after she'd moved out, his mom had crashed her car over on Highway 46. The police report indicated her car had drifted off the road and she'd overcorrected and lost control of her car. It had flipped several times.

She'd been pronounced dead at the scene.

Anna knew this part of the story. What she didn't know was the part Jake had learned three years ago, when his father died. It had changed everything.

"What?" Anna asked. "You looked so far away there for a minute. We were talking about how I'm sure the right woman can help you see that your family history shouldn't turn you against marriage."

He wasn't sure why he was going to tell her this, but how could he make her fully understand? But the words were spilling out before he could stop himself.

"When my dad died three years ago, you couldn't come for the funeral."

She frowned. "I know. I'm sorry, Jake. Hal was just so impossible when it came to you."

"God, he was obsessed with the notion that you and I had something going on. It was kind of crazy, huh?" He shook his head as he remembered the no-win situation. "I've never told you this, but after my dad died, I learned something that floored me. It changed me. In fact, it turned my entire childhood and upbringing into a lie."

Anna sat up, grimacing as she did so, but she turned her full attention on him.

"What was it, Jake?"

He took a deep breath, suddenly regretting opening up this line of conversation. But they'd come this far and Anna was the one person he'd always trusted with all his secrets. He'd managed to keep this one to himself for three years.

"My mom didn't simply leave our family out of the blue. She had a good reason—my father had been seeing Peggy for at least a year when my mom found out about their affair. He kept their relationship hidden for two years, or at least he kept her away from my brothers and me, but he married her. You know how she made our lives hell when we were growing up. And then after the funeral, she couldn't rest until she made sure that my brothers and I knew about her affair with our father."

Anna's jaw dropped.

"All those years, we thought my mom was the one who'd walked away from us, and my dad let us believe she was the villain, even after she died, when all that time our father had been living a double life. I just can't get over what a screwed-up situation it was, and then there's the added guilt of how my brothers and I vilified our mother because we believed she'd walked out on us.

"That's why I don't want to get married, because their bad marriage and my dad's deceit ultimately turned our childhood into one big lie."

She sat there watching him, taking it all in. "I'm so sorry that happened to you and your brothers. With both of your parents gone, I'm sure it must feel like a whole lot of unresolved business. But, Jake, I am imploring you not to let it continue to rob you of something that could be incredibly good for you."

* * *

The following week, Anna was definitely on the mend. Her sprained wrist was still tender, but it was feeling remarkably better. She'd done light duty to give it a chance to heal. Now she was nearly back up to speed. Since she'd only been at the hospital for a little over a month, she wanted to make sure she pulled her own weight. She didn't have time for an injury, but she was heartened when her coworker, Patty, had assured her that she and the others on the OB floor were happy to pick up the slack, such as carrying heavy supply baskets and equipment.

Even if they leaned a little heavy on the gossip sometimes, Anna believed that they truly had her back, even in the short time she'd been working at Celebration Memorial Hospital.

Of course, nothing came without a price. They were more curious than ever about what was happening with her and Dr. Lennox.

"Nothing is happening," Anna told them.

And Patty maintained that the jazz festival lip-lock certainly didn't look like *nothing*.

"Sorry to disappoint you, but he and I are just friends. I've known him all my life."

Patty and Marissa exchanged dubious glances. "Looks more like friends with benefits to me," Patty said.

"No. It's not like that. If you don't believe me, maybe this will change your minds—we both have dates tonight. In fact, we are double-dating."

"Are you dating each other and going out with another couple, or..." Marissa asked.

"Or. He has a date and I have a date. Since our dates are both this evening, we thought it would work if we all went out together. You know how blind dates are. Anything to make them easier."

Patty's eyes grew large. "Did you fix Dr. L up on a blind date?"

"I did." Anna had the sinking feeling she'd better steer this conversation in another direction. It was getting a little too personal; Jake wouldn't be very happy if word got out and he traced it back to Anna as the original source.

"If you're looking for candidates, keep me in mind," said Marissa.

"Hey, I have dibs," cried Patty.

"You're both crazy," said Anna. "But only in the best way."

That evening as they walked into the bar inside Bistro St. Germaine to wait for their dates, Vicki Bright and Burt Jewell, Anna was hyperaware of the light pressure of Jake's hand on the small of her back. It was more possessive than if he'd simply walked beside her, but not quite as intimate as if he held her hand or put his arm around her. But why was she even thinking about that kind of closeness?

The bistro—where Emily worked, but she was off tonight—was an upscale spot with floor-to-ceiling glass doors that folded open so that the bar and casual dining area spilled out onto the sidewalk outside the restaurant. The more formal dining room had tables in the back that were covered with crisp white linen tablecloths and sported small votive candles and vases hosting single red rosebuds.

As they approached the maître d' stand, the soft strains of a jazz quartet and muted conversation buzzed in the air.

Anna was glad she'd worn her black dress—it wasn't too dressy, but it still had an air of sophistication.

They were meeting their dates at the restaurant. The one thing to which Anna had held firm during this bet with Jake was that she would meet her blind dates at the location. She didn't want strangers picking her up. What if the guys were real duds? Or turned out to be stalkers? Still, Anna made no apologies about playing by her own rules.

Vicki had driven herself tonight, too. Because of that, Jake and Anna had ridden together.

The bar was buzzing with people. Jake and Anna managed to grab the last two open seats. Anna ordered a glass of merlot and Jake had a beer.

As they waited for their drinks, Anna asked, "What do you need me to do to help you with the Fourth of July party? Because you're going to be out of town next week, aren't you?"

"I leave tomorrow."

"Oh, really? I didn't realize the conference was so soon."

Hospital CEO Stan Holbrook had personally asked Jake if he would attend a medical conference on research and development and bring back the information to share with the rest of the staff. It was proof positive that Jake was on Stan's radar and it seemed like another step toward securing the chief hospitalist position.

"Yes, I decided to fly in a couple of days early so I could spend some time with Bob Gibson, my mentor from med school. He's retired and living in New Orleans now. I haven't seen him in years."

"Sounds like fun. Are you boys going to tear up Bourbon Street?"

Jake laughed. "Hardly. That's a little too spring break for me. Besides, Bob hasn't been doing very well lately. He's been having some health problems. But he sounded good when I talked to him. He suggested we grab some dinner and then go listen to some jazz over on Frenchmen Street. It's quite a bit lower-key than Bourbon Street. After that, it will be all medical conference all the time and I won't have time for much sightseeing. But I'll bring back some Mardi Gras beads for you if you want."

"That's sweet of you, Jake. Only if you have time to get them. Please don't make a special trip into the drunken debauchery just for me."

"I would go to the ends of the earth for you."

There was something in his eyes that made her melt a little inside. It was an odd feeling because this was *Jake*. She wasn't quite sure what to say. They'd always kidded around, but somehow this didn't feel like a joke. A lot of things had felt different in the month since she'd been back in Celebration.

Or maybe she was reading too much into it after that kiss, which certainly hadn't felt like a joke—

"I see Burt," Jake said, staring at a point over Anna's shoulder. "That must be Vicki."

Anna turned around and saw her friend Vicki— actually, she was Emily's friend. Emily had suggested Jake and Vicki might hit it off since she was smart, pretty and a busy, professional woman who seemed to be more committed to her work as an attorney than hunting for a husband.

Vicki was standing in the restaurant's entryway, engaged in deep conversation with a bald man who was a little on the short and pudgy side. The two of them were already engaged in conversation, talking and laughing animatedly like old friends.

"Is that Burt in the brown jacket?" Anna said. "If so, the woman he's hugging is my friend, Vicki."

"Yep, that's Burt. Do they know each other?" Jake slid off of his bar stool and extended a hand to help Anna down.

"I hope so. If they didn't before they do now."

Come to find out, they did know each other. They'd dated in high school, but had lost touch. What a small world, they marveled. It was a wonder that they hadn't crossed paths before this since they both lived in the Dallas area and Vicki was an attorney who practiced family law; Burt was a psychologist specializing in family counseling. They may even have had clients in common.

Anna watched the years melt away for them right before her eyes. And she was happy for them, even if all branches of conversation seemed to lead back to *remember that time when...* or legal/family counseling shop talk. Even when Anna or Jake tried to steer the conversation toward something more inclusive, it managed to wind back around to a precious moment Vicki and Burt had shared.

Finally, after they had finished their entrées, Anna and Vicki excused themselves to the ladies' room.

"What a small world, isn't it?" Vicki said. "Burt was my big love back in the day. We lost touch after I found out that he'd gotten married. He's divorced now."

"*Whew*, what a relief," Anna joked. "Since he's here for a blind date. You know, the two of you should get together. Seems like that old spark is still there."

She was sincere and she certainly hadn't meant to sound snarky or jealous—God, no, she wasn't jealous. She was inspired by the sweet rekindling of long-lost love. But Vicki must have interpreted it as a dig because she turned and looked at Anna, her mouth forming a perfect, soundless O.

"We have been so rude tonight," she said. "Anna, I'm so sorry. The way Burt and I have monopolized the conversation tonight is just inexcusable."

Anna put a hand on Vicki's arm. "You have nothing to apologize for. I would love nothing more than to see you and Burt get to spend more time together. Really. I mean it. There's nothing like a second chance at love."

"Well, I feel just terrible. You went to all the trouble to fix me up with your friend, Jack—"

"Actually, it's *Jake*."

Vicki covered her face with her hands. "I'm sorry. I'm really batting a thousand tonight, aren't I?"

"The heart wants what the heart wants." Anna smiled

at her reassuringly. "You have absolutely no reason to be sorry."

As they made their way back to the dining room, Anna wasn't sure if the relief she felt was because she wouldn't have to make excuses at the end of the night about why she couldn't see Burt again or if it was because Vicki and Jake would not have a second date.

Chapter Seven

Jake had gotten back into town late the previous night after his trip to New Orleans for the weeklong medical conference. He hadn't slept well. Actually, he hadn't slept well the whole time he was gone. His mind kept wandering to places it had no business dwelling.

And then, *dammit*, once he'd gotten back into town, he was tempted to drive straight over to Anna's house, because all he could think about was how he'd missed her.

Thank God common sense reigned, because he'd gone home and crawled into his own bed instead of going to her.

The first thing this morning, he'd texted her and asked her to meet him for lunch in the hospital courtyard.

Our table on the patio? he'd asked.

The table that was shaded by a large oak tree. The day was mild and clear, the perfect opportunity to sit outside and get some fresh air.

I'm so there, she'd responded. I've missed you. But then she'd qualified it with, We need to firm up July 4 party plans.

Now, as he walked toward her, he couldn't get over how beautiful she looked, sitting at the table, soaking up the sunshine. Her auburn hair was pulled back off her face and when she looked at him and smiled, he saw that she wore hardly any makeup. She didn't need it. She looked fresh and gorgeous without it.

"Hey stranger," he said as he set his tray on the table. "Anyone sitting here?"

"I was saving that seat for someone very special," she said.

He leaned in and kissed her on the cheek. "How's it going? How's your wrist feeling?"

"No problem," she said, moving it in a circle. "It's pretty much back to normal now. What's in there?" Anna nodded toward the white plastic bag he carried.

"I brought you something." He pushed it toward her. "Open it."

She cast a questioning glance at him and he smiled at her.

"I think you're going to like it."

She opened the bag and peered inside. Then reached in and pulled out several strands of Mardi Gras beads and a CD.

"What's this? Wait a minute—is this what I think it is?"

"You won't believe this, but that reggae-jazz fusion group we saw at the jazz festival was playing at The Spotted Cat, a music club on Frenchmen Street. What are the chances? Here's the CD they were talking about at the jazz festival."

Anna held up the CD and examined it. "Are you kidding me? That's crazy. And I love it."

She was scanning the back cover of the CD. "'Love is in the Air' is on it." He noticed a flicker in her eyes.

"Yeah, there it is. I like that song." He noticed that she didn't meet his gaze. Suddenly, she was acting a little shy.

Keeping it light, he said, "I had to drag myself through the drunken debauchery to get those beads for you."

"Thank you for compromising yourself for me," she said, fingering the beads. She set the CD on the table and looked thoughtful as she traced the letters spelling out the name with her finger.

For a moment, the craziest thought crossed his mind—he would do anything in the world for her. What was happening between them? Because suddenly everything seemed different and the weirdest part was, it didn't scare him. Neither did the fact that, right or wrong, he wanted to explore it a little more. He'd realized that over the week that he was gone.

"Oh, my God, did you get a card from Vicki and Burt?" she asked, suddenly seeming more like herself.

It took a moment for the names to register. "Oh, right, Burt and Vicki. Hearing their names together threw me."

"Well, wait until you hear this. Did you get anything in the mail from them this week?"

"I had the post office hold my mail while I was at the conference. They're delivering it today. Why? What did you get from them?"

"You have to see this." She fished in her purse and then handed him a peach-colored envelope that was nearly the same hue as her scrubs. "I'm sure you got one, too, but I want to see your face when you read this."

He squinted at her, hoping for a hint about what was inside. She looked as if she could hardly contain herself.

"Open it," she said, gesturing toward the envelope.

Jake pulled out a white card and blinked at the picture on the front. It was Vicki Bright and Burt Jewell. Underneath the black-and-white photo, spelled out in bold, black letters, it said,

We're getting married!
Save the Date: December 24, 2015.

Jake's mouth fell open. Then he laughed. "Is this a joke? They just reconnected with each other *a week* ago. Can you even get printing done that fast, much less propose, address cards and mail them out? They obviously had a lot of catching up to do after we left them at the restaurant."

"Funny thing is, I thought Vicki didn't want to get married," said Anna. "Emily told me she was too immersed in her quest to make partner at her law firm. But it's not as if they just met. They were high school sweethearts. Maybe she was waiting for him?"

His stomach tightened in a weird way and as he looked into her beautiful blue eyes, there was that feeling again. The two of them had been separated for a decade and Anna had only been back in his life full-time for one month, but after all these years it seemed as if a lot had changed. Changed for the better. And he wasn't quite sure what to do with these feelings. One thing that remained constant was they wanted different things from life. She wanted marriage and a family. He…wasn't so sure.

"Well, we know we can set up the perfect couple," he said. "Apparently just not for each other."

"Don't count me out just yet. I have someone in mind to fix you up with for the July Fourth party. Cassie Davis, that nurse on the second floor."

"Cassie? Oh…she's nice. And pretty. She sort of reminds me of you in a way."

Anna threw him a look.

"Oh, well, poor Cassie. I guess that means you're not interested."

Why had he said that? Or at least, why had he said it that way? It wasn't a slam. Any guy would be lucky to have Anna. Unfortunately, the jackasses of the world, like her ex, always seemed to come in and mess things up for the good guys. Jake wondered if in her eyes he fell into that jackass category, dating beautiful women who weren't marriage material, so, a few months down the road, he could walk away with his bachelorhood intact.

"I didn't mean anything bad by it," he said.

Tell her. Tell her that a man would be lucky to have her love.

But the words stuck in his throat and then he convinced himself that he'd better quit while he was ahead, or at least before he dug himself in deeper.

"I don't know if it's a good idea to date someone I work with. Look how messy it got after people saw us together at the jazz festival."

Anna's right brow shot up the way it always did just before she made a smart-mouthed comment about something. But then, it was as if she stopped herself before she said what was on her mind. He realized what he'd said might've sounded as though he was calling their night at the jazz festival a date.

It wasn't.

Not technically.

God, he didn't want to pressure her.

No, if it had been a date…what would he have done differently? He might've asked her if she was available earlier, rather than just showing up at her house. But one of the things he loved about her—about *them*—was that they were spontaneous. They didn't have to schedule fun. Fun seemed to follow them wherever they went. It was as natural as—

"You're welcome to invite her, if you'd like," he said. "But how about we don't bring dates to the party? It's a lot of pressure."

He hoped that didn't sound wrong. Even though he didn't know how else it could sound.

"I mean, you can bring a date if you want. But I think I want to go solo to this one. Since we're cohosting. It might be easier."

"If I didn't know better, I might think you were asking me to be your date."

Her eyes sparkled as she sat there watching him. She was baiting him, but he wasn't going to bite.

"Even better, I was thinking Cassie could be your date for the wedding. Really, she's perfect, if you think about it. Stan Holbrook knows her. He thinks highly of her. Everyone does."

"If everyone loves her so much, why is she still available?"

She clucked her tongue at him and wrinkled her nose.

"Watch what you say there, buddy. You make it sound like she has some sort of defect. She's a good catch. Don't forget, you and I are *available*. Does that mean we're defective, too?"

"Of course not."

"Okay, then. Take Cassie to the wedding?"

"If it will get you off my back." He smiled at her to make sure she knew he was joking.

Sort of.

"Okay, good. That's one thing off my plate. You do realize I'm a step ahead of you here. Even though the dates with Vicki and Cheryl didn't work out, Cassie is a keeper. Or at least someone you don't need to toy with."

"I don't toy with women. Especially not women I work with."

She shrugged as if she were giving him that point. "You need to fix me up with someone decent. I mean, Joe and Burt are nice guys, decent guys, but they weren't for me. Obviously. So you'd better bring your A-game for this one. I don't want to be the third wheel on your wedding date."

He wouldn't mind her being the third wheel. No, actually it crossed his mind that maybe it would be a better idea if they went to the wedding together. But he knew what she would say to that. By the grace of God, things had not gotten weird after the kiss. He needed to rein it in a bit before his luck ran out.

Sitting here, looking at her, fresh-faced and lovely, his body was telling him exactly what he wanted—her, in her bed, with nothing between them but their feelings. But then reality crashed the party, reminding him that she wanted—she *deserved*—so much more than he could offer her.

For a moment, he let his mind go there. He was crazy about her in a way that he had never felt about any other woman in his life. Would it be so bad? Of course it wouldn't. But he had to stop pushing the envelope with her. If he kept on, he was bound to hurt her. Ruin everything between them.

And that was the last thing he wanted to do.

"Let me think about a date for you," he said.

Dylan Tyler came to mind. He had a good career and he and Anna had both found each other attractive—as they'd stated at the jazz festival. But he wasn't going to lie to himself. The fact that Dylan and Anna might be just a little too perfect for each other made him uncomfortable. Did he really want to tempt fate?

What the hell did it even mean, that he was thinking that way?

If he knew what was best for both of them, he would say goodbye now.

* * *

At least forty people had turned out for the party. Apparently, Jake's annual shindig had become something of an institution. One of the reasons his house was the perfect place for this party was that fireworks from at least three different local shows were visible over the water.

Since Anna had been in San Antonio until last month, and because Hal had been so funny about her friendship with Jake, this was the first year she'd been able to attend his infamous party, much less be involved in helping him host.

"Hey, Anna, you and Jake throw a great party," said her sister, Emily, who was sitting around a fire pit with Ty and Ben, two of Jake's three brothers, roasting marshmallows for s'mores. "I think they make a good team. Don't you, Ty?"

Emily could be such an instigator sometimes. She flashed a smile at Anna, then turned her charm on Jake's youngest brother, Ty. She could be a flirt *and* an instigator. Anna sat down on the arm of the Adirondack chair Emily was in. Her sister's long brown hair hung in soft waves around her tanned shoulders. The aqua halter top she wore accentuated her blue eyes. The glow of the fire made her cheeks look rosier than usual. Or maybe it was simply the fact that she was in her glory, enjoying the sight of the younger Lennox brothers engaging in a subtle tug-of-war for her attention.

"I'm glad you're having fun," Anna said.

"She's right, you know," said Ty. "Jake's Fourth of July parties are always good, but you've helped him kick it up another notch this year. I think there's something to this pairing."

Anna nudged her sister's leg, in a thanks-a-lot-for-getting-this-started gesture. "Well, what you see is what you get. You know Jake and I have always been good buddies."

"I think you two are good for each other," said Ben. "He seems so much happier lately—since you moved back."

The idea sent Anna's spirits soaring, despite the fact that she sensed a conspiracy.

Ty was a good-looking guy. He was an EMT, the kind who might be featured on the cover of a first-responders calendar. He'd always had a thing for Emily, but she'd always viewed him as a brother. Maybe that was the thing about knowing somebody since their paste-eating kindergarten years. Sometimes it was hard to see past the old and into the possibilities.

"Where is Luke tonight?" Anna asked. "I thought he'd be here."

She glanced at her sister. Emily had always had a thing for Luke Lennox. Wasn't it just the grand irony that Ty seemed to be attracted to Emily, but Emily was interested in Luke? And Luke... Who knew where Luke's head and heart were these days? He'd been pretty scarce since Anna had been back. He was nearly as bad as his older brother when it came to loathing commitment.

"Are they giving you a hard time?" As if on cue, Jake walked up beside Anna and rested a hand on her shoulder. Her skin prickled under his touch, and she held her breath, hoping Emily wouldn't start asking why she and Jake were trying to fix each other up…when the obvious answer was right there in front of them.

Well, that's what Emily would say.

And Anna couldn't believe she was even letting her mind go there. She and Jake were obviously wrong for each other. They wanted completely different things out of life, even if this attraction did seem to pull them both toward a middle ground where they could meet… but for how long? And to what end?

"Do you really think I'd let them get away with that?" Anna said.

She'd been working on the decorations and setting up for the party since midmorning. She'd strung stars-and-stripes bunting along the back of the house and festooned the tables with red, white and blue tablecloths, and napkins and centerpieces made of white hydrangeas and small flags arranged in vases that looked like mini-washtubs.

This was the first chance she'd had to slow down all day. She'd worked up until the guests had started arriving. Then she'd quickly changed from her shorts into her red sundress and she'd played hostess, greeting everyone, fetching drinks and doing her best to make them feel at home. Her stomach growled a stern reminder that she hadn't eaten much that day.

Now dusk was settling over the backyard. It was just about time to bring out the giant flag cake she'd made—a sheet cake with whipped cream icing, adorned with strawberries and blueberries to form the stars and stripes on the flag. She'd have just enough time to grab a bite and serve the cake before the fireworks started.

"I'm starving," she said to Jake. "I have got to get something to eat. Would you care to join me?"

"I'd love to," he said. "Let's grab some food and go down to the dock."

"The dock, hmm?" Emily muttered. "That sounds romantic."

Anna stepped on her sister's foot as she stood.

"Ouch!" Emily said. "That hurt."

"Mmm-hmm." Anna shot her sister a sweet smile. "I intended for it to. Mind your manners."

As they walked toward the food table, Jake asked, "What was that about?"

Anna shrugged and pretended to be much more focused on the barbecue than was really necessary. "Oh, you know how Emily can be. I was just keeping her in line."

"What's she getting you all riled up about now?"

Jake's voice was deep and ridiculously alluring. Anna slanted a glance at him.

"She's gotten it into her head that we shouldn't fix each other up."

Jake raised a questioning eyebrow, but something in his gaze seemed to say he knew what she was going to say next.

"She thinks you and I should date," Anna said. "She always has."

Jake shot her a lopsided smile that reminded her of the times when he used to triple-dog-dare her to do things she would've never tried on her own.

Or maybe she was simply imagining it.

Anna looked away, training her focus on the food, inhaling the delicious scent of barbecue and trying to ignore how her stomach had suddenly twisted itself into a knot. She helped herself to the barbecued ribs Jake had spent all day slow-cooking, a scoop of potato salad and some baked beans.

"Want a beer to go with that?" Jake asked.

He looked *good*, standing there in his blue jeans and bright blue polo shirt. Her stomach did a little flip, which she tried to convince herself was hunger.

But hunger for what, exactly?

The flames from the tiki torches cast shadows on his face, accentuating his strong jaw line and full lips. He was sporting that sexy-scruffy five-o'clock shadow that Anna had become inexplicably fond of. He fished a bottle of the micro-brew he'd picked up for the party out of the cooler and held it up for her to see.

"Yes, please. That sounds wonderful."

They'd been so busy facilitating that they hadn't had a chance to say much to each other, much less enjoy a beer together.

Jake grabbed another bottle out of the cooler and turned toward the dock.

She took her plate and followed him. It was one of the few unoccupied spaces, probably because it was set away from the food and festivities. Their friends were clustered in groups under the canopy of trees that stretched protectively over the large backyard. All the seats and places at the tables appeared to be occupied. In fact, people were sitting on the ground amidst the tiki torches and fire pit; everyone was talking and laughing and seemed to be having a great time. But right now, all Anna wanted was to find a quiet place away from the crowd where she could eat, and if that place happened to be on the dock, alone with Jake...all the better.

This was what she'd been missing all the years she'd been away. A lot of things had changed, but one thing that had become a tradition was that people loved to gather at Jake's house. She hadn't asked him, but she wondered if over the years his various girlfriends had played hostess. She made a note to rib him about it later.

But not now.

There wasn't time.

The sun was setting, and Anna knew if she didn't eat while she could, soon everyone would be shifting out from under the trees, toward the dock and the lakeshore to watch the fireworks. She didn't want to spend what little alone time they might have conjuring the ghosts of exes past.

For the first time that evening, as Anna sat there with Jake, she inhaled a full deep breath and relaxed.

On the dock, they sat side by side on the bench that overlooked the lake. The warm summer breeze must've blown out the tiki torch that Jake had lit earlier, because the only light came from the dusky twilight reflecting off the water.

He was sitting so close to her that his muscular biceps grazed her when he lifted his beer to take a sip.

All seemed right with the world as they sat next to each other listening to the symphony of cicadas, just as they had so often before. But this time, something felt different. There was a charge in the air. No matter how Anna tried to ignore it or explain it away or put herself on notice, she didn't care that it was a bad idea to allow herself to be drawn in by this strange, new magnetic pull that was so strong between them.

"It seems like everyone is having a great time," said Jake.

She was acutely aware that his knee had drifted over and was pressing against hers, and she was doing nothing to put some much-needed space between them. She didn't intend to do anything.

"Yeah, they are. We should do this more often."

"Do what? Have a July Fourth party?"

She was just about ready to swat his arm for the sarcastic remark, but he said, "Or should we do *this* more often?" He gestured between them. "I'd vote for this, myself."

She felt shy all of a sudden, as if he were testing her wit…and she couldn't come up with a good comeback. All her words felt clunky and strange and wrong.

Or maybe he was calling her bluff?

It sure seemed like it when he trailed his finger along the tender underside of her arm. The feel of his hand on her was her touchstone, her anchor, the one thing in this world that simultaneously frightened her and made perfect sense.

He set down his beer and turned his body to face her. He was looking at her with an intensity that had her gripping the edge of the bench to keep from reaching for him.

Despite the summer breeze blowing across the lake, the heat between them flared. He was playing with her hair, and she reached out and touched his hand. It was just meant to be a passing touch—something to anchor her, but it seemed to ignite that spark.

She wasn't sure who moved first, but suddenly they were kissing each other.

He kissed her exactly the way she hoped he would: deliberate and intense, as if he wanted to prove to her that they were *that* good together. That it really was electric. That it hadn't been a fluke that night when he'd first kissed her at the jazz festival. Right there in front of everyone. In front of their coworkers and their neighbors and God. In the moment, she hadn't worried about who saw them or questioned them or talked about them. She didn't think she would ever worry about it. This was Jake. The guy who had always looked out for her. Protected her.

She was sure he was still that guy who cared about her more than the man she'd married had ever done. But she wasn't the blindly foolish woman who'd convinced herself for years that her feelings for her best friend were purely platonic.

No. She definitely wasn't that woman anymore.

In this moment, she was just a woman who wanted a man. *This man.* And the sizzling hot, extraordinary kiss he was giving her. She would consider the consequences later.

Or maybe she wouldn't.

Maybe she'd pretend there were no consequences to worry about.

Maybe she worried too much.

Jake was kissing her and nothing else mattered. This

dock was their own world for two, their own universe. It was vast and amazing. This kiss wasn't about weddings and children and happily-ever-afters that she could never have with him.

Stop thinking so much, Anna.

This kiss wasn't about friendship and history and knowing each other inside and out.

The only thing that mattered was that this felt amazing. It worked. *They worked.* They were good together.

She wanted it, and he did, too.

She fisted her hands into his shirt and felt the warm, solid weight of his body against hers. He leaned into her, even closer, his hands moving across her back, down her to her hips, then sliding back up her sides and pushing against the weight of her breasts. He lingered there, liking it, she hoped. As if silently answering her, he shifted his body just enough to move his hands in so he could explore and caress.

He made a low, deep sound in his throat and she felt the vibration of it all the way through her own body, like fireworks on the Fourth of July or the rumble of a night train steaming its way through the heat of summer.

She wanted to live in that dark, rich sound; she wanted it to pick her up and carry her far away from every thought or intrusion of reality that might come between them.

But then, without warning the kiss ended. He pulled those delicious lips away. It was so abrupt it was disorienting, like soaring through the inky, starry sky one moment and then free-falling back down to earth the next.

"I'm so sorry." He moved back, raking his hand through his hair, putting some distance between them.

"Why are you sorry? Don't be sorry, Jake."

"This wasn't supposed to happen again," he said. "I promised myself I wouldn't kiss you again."

"So you've been thinking about kissing me again?"

He nodded. "I haven't been able to get those lips of yours out of my head." He seemed a little subdued. Maybe even a bit contrite.

"It's okay. It's fine, really. Would it make a difference if I confessed that I was hoping you'd kiss me again?"

She just blurted out the words. It was only the truth, and why shouldn't she tell him the truth?

Why? Well, she had a long list of why's for not confessing this particular truth, but they didn't matter right now.

"You deserve someone so much better than me, Anna." He leaned back and seemed to be trying to put even more distance between them.

"I've never met anyone who treats me better than you do."

He shook his head, looking so remorseful that it nearly broke her heart. "Believe me, you could do *so* much better. You *should* do better than me...than this. Especially after Hal."

No. She wasn't having any part of that.

"Don't be so hard on yourself, Jake. Remember, I've had two years to work through my failed marriage. I didn't rush right into dating the day after it happened. Not even the day I signed my divorce papers. It took you to get me back out into the world, albeit kicking and screaming, but I'm glad you nudged me out there."

"Even though the two dates I've fixed you up on have been complete and utter failures?"

"That's right. I sprained my wrist with the first guy and the other one married my sister's friend. If I didn't know you better, I'd think you were setting me up to fail. Is that what happened? Or was it leading me here?"

His right brow shot up. She loved the way he looked. It made her smile. *He* made her smile.

"I guess you have conquered your fear of getting back out there in the dating world."

If not for him, she'd still be hiding away.

"And you're the one who helped me do that," she said. "You've reminded me that romance isn't necessarily synonymous with pain. Thank you for that."

"But God, what are we doing, Anna?"

"Jake, why won't you let me in?"

There was a full moon tonight and the reflection of it rising over the water flickered in his eyes. He looked at her for a long moment and she could almost hear the jumbled thoughts churning in his head as he tried to put them in order.

"You're such a good person, Anna." He sounded preoccupied and she might've jumped to the conclusion that he was trying to let her down easy, but his expression and his body language told a completely different story. He was leaning in again. "You deserve someone equally as good."

"Shut up." She pressed her finger to his lips. "Don't ruin this moment."

His gaze, smoldering and intense and completely at odds with his protests, locked with hers.

"You just have to promise me one thing," he said.

Running the pad of her index finger over his tempting bottom lip, her wrist rubbed against the sexy stubble on his cheeks. Her body reacted with a warming shiver. He opened his mouth and gently caught her finger between his teeth. Nipped at it and sucked on it for a moment.

It felt like she'd been waiting her entire life for this moment. Despite his words, he certainly didn't seem to be in a hurry to get away. *Yeah*, he wasn't going anywhere.

Not right now, at least.

"Anything," she said.

She wasn't going to let him tell her he wasn't good enough for her.

She knew what she wanted, and he'd just slipped his arms around her again.

"No regrets," he said.

"No regrets," she answered. "But tell me something. How do you know that you're not good for me—that we're not good together—if we've never…tried it out?" She whispered the proposition inches from those lips of his, letting the promise tease his senses. "I'll bet we could be very good…together. The only thing I'd regret is if I never knew for sure."

He drew in a ragged breath and she scooted onto his lap, feeling the rock-solid proof of his interest underneath her.

"God, Anna, you're killing me," he murmured. His

breath was hot and he seemed more than a little *bothered* by the way he adjusted the angle of his hips so that their bodies aligned through their clothing.

He murmured something under his breath, but it was lost when he closed his mouth over hers and kissed her with a hunger that had him deftly turning her body so that she was straddling him.

It felt perfect, and dangerous, and maddeningly, temptingly delicious, awakening in her a hunger that she feared she might have to satisfy right here on the dock—with the guests behind the trees, only a few yards away. All someone had to do was walk down the path and around the corner and they would be discovered. But she didn't care. She wasn't thinking of problems or reasons why not, or second-guessing her actions or his reactions. It just felt so darn right, and that was all she cared about.

That thought cut the line that tethered her to reality and she let herself drift out on the tide of his kiss.

A few minutes later—or maybe it was hours, who knew?—Jake's phone rang. At first, he ignored it, but then it rang again.

"You'd better get that," Anna murmured. "It sounds like someone is trying to get you."

He wasn't on call, but if there was a big emergency at the hospital, Jake would've been among the first to be notified. Still tingling with awareness, Anna eased herself off of Jake's lap to give him some room. He fished his phone out of his pocket, but by the time he'd pulled it out, the phone signaled a voice mail.

"It's a 504 area code. That's New Orleans. Sorry, but I should pick up this message."

"Of course," she said.

As Jake listened to the voice mail, Anna watched his features contort into a mask of shock and disbelief. Then he stared at his phone for a moment before looking up at Anna.

"Is everything okay?" she asked.

He shook his head. "No. It's not. Bob Gibson passed away this morning."

Chapter Eight

Despite how strong Jake had tried to be, he'd ended up asking Anna, Emily and his brothers to tend to the guests while he stepped out for a few moments. Anna empathized with what he must've been feeling after receiving the news of Bob's death. Even though Jake was no stranger to personal loss after the death of both his parents, it never got easier.

After the fireworks ended, the guests began saying their goodbyes and calling it a night. It was a Saturday, but some of them, including Anna, had to work tomorrow. After all, the hospital was open 24/7. It didn't operate on bankers' hours.

Since she had to work, Emily, Ty and Ben had offered to tend to the basic cleanup—gathering trash and extinguishing tiki torches and the fire pit so that Anna could go home and get some sleep.

Her lips still tingled from his kiss. She didn't want to leave. She wanted to be there for Jake when he returned, but after thinking about it and weighing everything that had happened that night, she decided that maybe it was better to give him a little space. She'd call him tomorrow. Maybe ask him to go for a run after she got off work.

She was supposed to have Sunday dinner at her parents' house. Maybe she'd see if he wanted to come along. Lord knew he'd spent more than a few Sundays at her family's dinner table when they were growing up. Maybe going back to the comfort of the past would help him feel better.

The last thing she expected when she turned onto her street was to see his car in her driveway. But there he was, sitting in the car. It was almost eleven o'clock.

By the time she parked and let herself out of the car, he was standing there.

"How long have you been here?" she asked.

"Not too long," he said. "I'm sorry I bolted. I needed to clear my head."

She held up her hands. "No apologies needed. Come on in."

He nodded.

Once they got inside, he sat down on the couch and she went to the refrigerator and got two beers.

"Are you okay?" she asked as she handed one to him and settled herself on the couch next to him.

He rested his hand on the back of the couch and stared up at the ceiling, looking thoughtful.

"It's strange," he said, "to think that Bob is gone. He was so alive last week." Jake shook his head. "Being a doctor, you'd think I'd get used to the fact that people die and life goes on. But it never gets easier."

"I guess that's why it's important to live in the moment and appreciate the people in your life while they're there," she said.

"You're right. As I was driving around, I was thinking about what you said. About why I won't let you in." His voice was a hoarse rasp. "I don't know why, but I want to try. I mean, your strength humbles me, Anna. I've been running from my monsters for so many years. You don't run. You face your biggest terrors head-on. I don't know if I can be that strong—but…" His voice trailed off.

"Jake, listen to me. You need to hear what I'm saying to you." She cupped her hand under his chin and turned his face toward hers. Staring into his eyes, she said, "You're a good man, Jake Lennox. You need to accept that and believe it."

He caught her hand and brought it to his mouth, pressing a kiss into her palm. Then he slid an arm around her and closed the distance between them, brushing one light, hesitant kiss on her lips.

"This is different for me, Anna." His lips were mere inches from hers. "You are different for me."

"Are you saying that because you're trying to seduce me?"

He was familiar, yet different, for her. They were

picking up from where they'd left off on the dock, but at the same time, it felt brand-new. This was still Jake—the same big frame, the same dark hair setting off blue eyes as inviting as the Mediterranean. But he was changed. His body was tense; his face was flushed and way too serious. Desire laced with a little sadness colored his eyes a deeper shade of blue.

"I'm just picking up where we left off earlier. If that's okay…?"

She rested her hand on his shoulder, not saying it wasn't okay, but not giving him the green light either. Despite how she wanted to stop talking and just lose herself in him.

"Jake, I need to know… I know that this is different for us. But we can't seem to keep our hands off each other. And that's not a problem. It's definitely *not* a problem. I just need to know… Really, it's not. I just need to know…what are we doing?"

He looked her square in the eyes.

"I'm exactly where I want to be, Anna, and with the person I desire. Doesn't that tell you what we're doing… or what we're about to do?" His lips were mere inches from hers. "I want to make love to you, Anna Adams. Tell me that you want that, too."

"Oh, I want you, too, Jake. You have no idea."

She kissed him, wanting to make sure there was absolutely no doubt in his mind exactly how okay it was.

Then he leaned in and closed the rest of the distance between them. Then they fell into a kiss, arms wrapped around each other; his hands trailing down her back to cup her bottom, her hands in his hair, desperately pulling him closer, both of them impatient and ravenous as they devoured each other.

Anna had unleashed a want in him that rendered him desperate for something he never knew he needed. This was exactly how he imagined her body would feel. Now, he was greedy for her, needing to know every inch of her, eager to bury himself deep inside her.

She took his hand and led him to the one place in her house he had never been—her bed. Her bedroom was feminine and fashionable. A king-size bed sported a blue-and-yellow bedspread, turned down over soft white cotton sheets. There was a dresser and matching nightstand that held a table lamp, but he didn't turn it on after they stumbled into the room, clinging to each other as if their next breath depended on it.

How many nights since she'd been back in Celebration had he held her in his dreams, subconsciously breathing in her scent, taking possession of her body, loving her with his mind and his heart as he slept?

How was it that he was just admitting this to himself?

He unclipped her hair and dug his hands into the heavy auburn mass of it. Then he walked her backward until he could feel the bed behind her legs. As he eased her down onto the mattress, he buried his face in her hair, breathed in the scent of her—that delicious smell of flowers, vanilla and amber. A fragrance that was so intimate and familiar. Yet the newness of it hit him in a certain place that rendered him weak.

Smoothing a wisp of hair off her forehead, he kissed

the place where it had lain; then he searched her eyes, needing to make sure she was still okay with this.

"Make love to me, Jake," she answered before he could even say the words.

He inhaled a shuddering breath. As he pulled her into his arms, a fire ignited and he melted into the heat of her body. Relishing the warmth of her and the way she clung to him, he cradled her face in his palms and kissed her softly, hesitating, as he silently gave her one last chance to ask him to stop, to leave, to walk away from what was about to happen.

As if she sensed his hesitation, she pulled him into a long, slow kiss.

"Relax," she said. "I won't break. I promise. *No regrets*, Jake. Remember?"

For a moment, he looked at her in the dusk. The only light in the room was cast by a slim slice of light from the other part of the house and the glow of the full moon filtering in through the slanted blinds.

"Your lips drive me crazy," he muttered. "They have since that night I first kissed you. How is it that we've known each other for so many years and it took all this time for me to realize this addiction? Now, I look at that bottom lip of yours and it just makes me crazy."

He drew her lip into his mouth and she kissed him with urgency and demand as she tugged at his shirt, yanking it free from his pants. The move sent a rush spiraling through him. He felt the silk of her hands as they slipped under his shirt and up his back, turning his skin to gooseflesh. He couldn't stifle a groan.

He pressed his lips to her collarbone, exploring the

smooth, delicate ridge, and lingering over the hollow between her shoulder and throat. He stopped when he reached the top of her dress.

She made an impatient noise. So he found the hem of her skirt and began pulling it up, easing her body up and slightly off the mattress so that he could rid them of one of the barriers that stood between them.

"You're so beautiful," he whispered as he eased it over her head.

She lay there in just her panties, since she hadn't worn a bra beneath her sundress.

She tugged off his shirt. He sank back down beside her, tracing his fingertips down the slender column of her throat, splaying his hand to touch both beautiful breasts and then sliding it down to gently graze her stomach with his fingertips. When he reached the top edge of her panties, he slid his fingers beneath the silk to find her center. She gasped as his fingers opened her and slipped inside her. A rush of red-hot need spiraled through him and he nearly came undone with her as he watched her go over the edge.

As he slid her panties down, it was as if she sensed his own need. She made haste of unbuckling his belt and unbuttoning his jeans. Before he tossed his pants away, he pulled a condom from his wallet and sheathed himself. When they were finally free of the last barrier between them, his arms encircled her. He held her so close he could hear her heart beat. He shut out everything else but that sound and the need that was driving him to the brink of insanity.

All he wanted was *her*.

Right here. Right now.

Not the past.

Not the future.

The present.

Right here. Right now.

She pulled him even closer so that the tip of his hardness pressed into her. He urged her legs apart and buried himself inside her with a deep thrust.

As his own moan escaped his lips, his gaze was locked on hers. He slid his hands beneath her bottom, helping her match his moves in and out of her body until they both exploded together.

He held her close, both of them clinging to each other as the aftershocks of their lovemaking gradually faded. As they lay there together, sweaty and spent, Jake was still reveling in the smoothness of her skin, the passion in her eyes, the way they'd fit together so perfectly… She took his breath away. What they had right now was damn near perfect. And if it weren't for the fact that it scared him to death, he might've felt like he'd come home.

Had Hal been right? Had she been in love with Jake all along but just hadn't realized it?

Because Anna had never felt fireworks the likes of which she'd just experienced with Jake.

Her body still thrummed.

She lay with Jake in her bed for what seemed like hours, lost in the rhythm of his breathing. He was sleeping on his stomach with one arm thrown protectively over her middle, sacked out, sound asleep. Anna lay there frozen, the realization of what had just happened taking on gargantuan proportions in her brain.

Now what?

Looking back, she knew they'd been on a trajectory for what had happened tonight ever since Jake had come to San Antonio to rescue her. He'd packed her up, moved her back to Celebration. Now they'd crossed that line and she feared her worst nightmare might be waiting to jump out at her with dawn's first glimmer: that everything would be different now between Jake and her. That Hal had been right all along.

Had he somehow hit on something to which Anna had been so clueless? Or worse, had she simply been in denial all these years? She'd always prided herself on knowing herself—who she was, what she wanted and how to get it. She'd always known what was *real*.

How was it that she was here with Jake, feeling this dichotomy of emotions? She wanted to be here, there was no doubt about that. But *should* she be here? That was the question that turned everything on its axis.

She shifted her body so she could turn her head to the right and look at him as he slept. Jake's face was inches from hers. He was sleeping soundly, the sleep of the innocent, as if he didn't have a care in the world. Based on the pleasant look on his features, he might open his eyes and smile at her and tell her this thing that had happened between them was good. Hell, it wasn't just good; it was great. They were great together.

But one other thing Anna knew about herself was that she was a realist. She never kidded herself about important matters. She may have been the last to know about Hal's affair, but once she'd learned the truth—saw the proof in black-and-white in front of her eyes on that computer screen—not once had she tried to pretend it was anything else other than what it was: betrayal.

So, now, as she lay here watching this beautiful man—this man who was her best friend, this man who was *Jake*—sleep with his arm thrown over her middle, she knew she couldn't ignore the truth: life as they'd known it had just irreparably changed.

A swarm of butterflies unfurled in her stomach, but she wasn't sure what she was supposed to do about them.

It took Jake a couple of seconds to remember where he was when he opened his eyes. He rolled over onto his elbow and saw Anna. He was with her. In her bed. She was sleeping peacefully beside him.

And it all came back to him.

He'd fallen asleep, but he wasn't sure how long he'd been out.

He glanced around the room and located a digital alarm clock that glowed cobalt blue in the darkness.

Five minutes until four. In the morning.

Awareness of her sleep-warmed, naked body so close woke every one of his senses. He fought the urge to move closer, pull her to him and make love to her again. God, how he wanted to, but—

God, if he didn't know what was good for him—or maybe he should focus on how bad it would be for him…for *them*—he'd give in to this weakness and stay right here next to her.

But he couldn't.

He should leave now before the sun came up and he and Anna were forced into saying awkward good-mornings and goodbyes. He gently eased himself off the bed, moving slowly so as not to wake her. He gathered his clothes and went out to the hall bathroom where he dressed.

When he stepped back out into the hall, he saw Anna clad in a robe and framed in her bedroom doorway.

"Where are you going?" Her voice sounded small.

"I was going home."

"You don't have to leave." His arm settled around her middle again and he nuzzled his nose into her neck.

"Anna… I have to go."

Oh, hell. This was the awkward moment he'd dreaded.

"Are you okay?"

"Yes. Fine. Great, I mean."

Liar.

"Jake? Were you just going to leave without waking me?"

"Why would I wake you?" He knew she had to work in a few hours. She might have a hard time falling back asleep.

The look on her face was equal parts horror and disbelief. Obviously, he hadn't given the right answer. Crap.

"No regrets, right?"

That's what they'd promised each other. Now he wondered if in the heat of the moment she'd meant it, but now she was having second thoughts.

He cared about her.

He thought those protective feelings would edge out any possibility of regret. Kissing her had certainly erased the word *regret* from his vocabulary. Now, not only was the word back, but it seemed to be swimming in his blood. Yet he had no choice but to keep his word or risk ruining everything. In the moment, he'd had no idea that it would be so difficult to have *no regrets*.

She just stood there, blinking at him with sleepy eyes, clutching the lapels of her robe. She looked as if she wanted to shove the word *regret* up his left nostril.

"I didn't wake you because I know you're on the schedule tomorrow—er, later today—and think about how everyone will talk if you show up looking sleep-deprived."

She was still doing that frown-squint thing.

"I guess they wouldn't necessarily know I'd spent the night with you," he said.

He was trying to be funny. But somehow his words were making it worse. They sounded like excuses... that were full of regret. But for a fraction of a second, a traitorous part of him wanted to take her back to bed and show her the meaning of "no regrets."

Instead, he raked his hand through his hair as he stared toward the door.

Regret, the bastard, wasn't so easy for him to ignore either.

Standing there watching Jake walk toward the door, Anna felt very naked and exposed, and not just in the physical sense. But now was a heck of a time to worry about that, wasn't it?

Don't make this any weirder than it has to be.

Don't look back, only forward. Because if you're not going to let this one night of indiscretion ruin a perfectly good friendship, you're going to have to leave it in the past.

As she watched him walk away, she tried not to wonder if he'd ever spent the entire night with Miss Texas. How in the world could she have left without her underwear? And why did it feel as if she were the one doing the walk of shame?

"Will you at least let me make you some coffee?" she asked. "It will only take a few seconds."

He turned back to her, his hand on the front doorknob. "No. Thanks, though. You should go back to bed and get a little more sleep before work."

Sleep? Was he serious?

She glanced around her living room to keep from looking at him. Anywhere but him. Funny, how her own house could look both familiar and foreign at the same time. Would everything look different now that this had happened?

"I intend to," she said. But suddenly she was tired of tiptoeing around the crux of the matter. "Jake. We don't have to talk about this now, but we both know this shouldn't have happened. What were we thinking? No, just—"

She gave her head a little shake and held up her hand to indicate she didn't want him to answer that. Not right now.

She found the courage to hold his gaze, wanting to make sure he understood the gist of what she meant.

He nodded. "I need to go. Let's talk later. After we're both rested and thinking with clearer heads."

Her heart lurched madly, but then it settled into a still ache beneath her breastbone.

He already had the front door open, but he stopped in the threshold and turned around. She wasn't prepared for the pain she saw in his blue eyes.

"Anna, it's still me. We are still us. Let's not let anything change that, okay?"

That's exactly the point.

Jake was still Jake—the man who grew tired of lovers after a few months.

They were still them—chums who should've left well enough alone, keeping relations firmly in the friend zone.

When he stepped outside, he lingered on the porch and Anna moved to the door, unsure about whether she should give him a goodbye hug as she always used to do…or a kiss?

No, definitely not a kiss.

And apparently not a hug either, since he was already making his way down the stairs. The reality of this mess made her heart hurt.

Trying not to think about it, she gazed out the front door at her neighborhood bathed in the inky predawn. She didn't see it like this very often: still and peaceful, and, besides Jake, not a soul in sight.

Across the street, there was a basketball hoop on a stand. It stood like a sentry along the side of the driveway. In the manicured yard of the house to the right of that, kids' toys lay lifeless and untouched. In the distance, someone had left a porch light on. As Jake walked to his car, Anna inhaled a deep breath and smelled the scent of late-night laundry that lingered in the air. Fabric softener perfumed the muggy summertime air.

This was her life, not Jake's. Mr. Don't-Fence-Me-In would be an anomaly in this cozy, family-oriented neighborhood. He didn't want a wife to tie him down or kids who would complicate his bachelor lifestyle. He didn't even own his own house because he was still convinced that he would be leaving Celebration for bigger and better things in the future. Even if he got the chief hospitalist position, it didn't mean he would stay. In fact, he could parlay it into a better position elsewhere.

If Anna fell in love with him, she was doomed. He would never marry her and that meant—well, that meant he could break her heart. She'd been there, done that. She'd let Hal break her heart. She wasn't opening herself up to that kind of hurt again.

So that was that. End of story.

They'd made a mistake. Now it was time to salvage what was left.

They both just needed some space.

The car chirped and she could hear the locks disengage. The sound seemed to echo in the still of the night.

Before he got into the car, he repeated, "No regrets, right?"

"I know, Jake. Good night."

Chapter Nine

In less than twelve hours, Jake's life had gone to hell.

First, the news about Bob Gibson's death and then the ridiculous stunt with Anna. Word of Bob's death had come as such a shock—he'd looked fine last week. Sure, maybe he was moving a little slower than he had in the past, but everyone slowed down. How could it be that a person was on this earth and seemingly fine one minute and then the next minute…they were gone?

He'd turned to Anna for comfort. Because sometimes—most of the time—she felt like the only thing in his life that was real and solid and true. Now, he might have screwed that up, too.

He knew he'd been playing with fire when they'd kissed the first time. Then, not only had he kissed her again, but he'd ended up in her bed.

Three strikes and you're out.

But just as with the first time they'd kissed, attraction seemed to take over. When the magnet of her pulled at the steel in him, resisting seemed futile—for both of them.

Man up. When have you ever not been in control?

Maybe that's what scared him the most.

When had this change in the chemistry between them happened? Growing up, they'd edged close to that line once, but they'd decided right away that they made more sense as friends. Then they'd each gone away to separate colleges and it always seemed like one or the other of them was involved. Then Anna met Hal, married him and moved away. That had seemingly sealed their fate—even if they hadn't been consciously aware of it. After all, they'd been away from each other for the past ten years—four years of college and six years that encompassed Anna's marriage, separation and eventual divorce.

Now that she was free and back in Celebration, she was the same Anna he'd loved his whole life. Yet even thinking about the platonic *love* he'd had for her his whole life, everything had felt different in the weeks that she'd been back.

For a crazy split second, Jake wondered if he'd dodged long-lasting commitment with the women he'd dated because he'd been waiting for Anna. But the thought was ridiculous. How could he have been waiting for her when she was already married?

He shook off the absurd notion.

Thoughts like that were pinging around in his head,

keeping Jake awake long after he'd gotten home. He'd lain there in his cold, empty bed, tossing and turning, feeling the phantom touch of her on his skin, smelling her and alternating between mentally flogging himself for jeopardizing his relationship with the most important person in his life and trying to digest the reality of Bob's death.

His mentor was gone. Anna was upset.

And rightfully so. What the hell was wrong with him?

If anyone else had tried to take advantage of Anna that way, they would've had hell to pay. Jake would've made sure.

After tossing and turning for what seemed like hours, he'd showered, made a pot of coffee and dragged himself out to the dock for some fresh air. As the sun overtook the lifeless, gray sky, bringing it to life in a blaze of variegated splendor, the lake shone like pieces of a broken mirror reflecting his misery back at him.

So, what now? He still hadn't found the answers he was seeking. Everything was still as messed up and disjointed as it had been since he'd walked out the door of Anna's house this morning. She deserved more than he could offer, more than one night as friends with benefits. Because even if he wanted to try to give her more, he just couldn't trust himself for the long haul.

He'd been a product of a broken marriage. He'd been led through his parents' maze of lies—his mother leaving, but shouldering all the blame, his father turning out to not be the man Jake had thought he had been all those years. Hell, for his entire life.

Marriage had taken something good and drained all the life out of it. Even though it might've seemed as if he were copping out on Anna by taking this stance, she would thank him in the long run. She still believed in happily-ever-after and he'd damn sure see that she got nothing less.

He would make things right between them.

Somehow he would make things right.

Judging from where the sun was sitting in the eastern sky, it had to be well after eight o'clock. He needed to quit brooding and get up and do something constructive with his Sunday. Since Anna was working today, he'd see if she was free for dinner tonight. Then he'd check on flights back to New Orleans for Bob's funeral.

As he walked from the dock through the yard, he surveyed the evidence of last night's party: the canopy was still up, tables and chairs needed to be put away and there were still a few stray beer bottles. Not that he was complaining; he was grateful that someone had stepped in and done the majority of the cleanup...while he'd been with Anna.

And damn if she hadn't fit perfectly in his arms.

At that moment he hadn't given a rat's ass about anything else. She was the one person in the world who'd always been there for him—even across the miles and years, during the time they'd been apart. She'd never let him down.

Now, he had a sinking feeling he'd let her down in the worst way. He needed to talk to her and make sure she was okay. Because he wouldn't be okay until he knew she was.

Jake grabbed a couple of empty bottles that were in his path and threw them into the recycling bin that sat just outside the back door. He'd clean up the rest later, but now, he needed to talk to Anna.

He let himself in the back door of his house and found his phone on the kitchen counter. He started to text her, but he thought a voice mail might be better. Texts were so impersonal. Meaning and intention could get lost or misconstrued.

He clicked over to his phone's keypad and dialed Anna's number. He didn't expect her to pick up since she was working, and he was in the middle of composing a message when Anna answered.

"Jake?"

It took him a beat or two, but he pulled his thoughts together.

Keep it light. Keep it upbeat.

"Hey, stranger. I was calling to leave you a message, but I'm glad you picked up. What do you say to dinner tonight? I'll cook for us."

There was a pause on the line that stretched on a little longer than it should've.

"That sounds great, but I can't tonight. I'm busy. Besides, you don't owe me a consolation dinner, Jake. Really, you don't."

He leaned his hip against the kitchen counter, trying to decide if she was joking. He detected a hint of truth in her words.

Busy? As in a date?

Despite how badly he wanted to know, he wasn't about to ask her.

"What a coincidence, because I hadn't planned one single bite of consolation on tonight's menu. How about a rain check?"

She laughed and he was so relieved to hear that sound he closed his eyes for a moment to savor it.

"Yes, of course. That would be great. But, hey, I'm going for a run this afternoon after I get home from work." Her voice was soft and she sounded a little vulnerable. "You can join me if you want. Unless you're busy."

"You just turned down my invite to dinner. Of course I'm not busy.

"We can run and then I'll fix dinner for us. Consolation-free, you have my word," he said. "How can you say no?"

She was quiet for longer than she should've been and that made Jake uncomfortable.

"Oh, come on, Anna. Don't make me come to the hospital to do the Sadness Intervention Dance. Because I will. It will be humiliating as hell, but I will march right up there to the third floor and dance in front of the nurses' station. Then you'll get to explain it to Patty and Marissa."

"Look, I really do have plans later this evening, but come run with me. We need to talk. Meet me downtown in the park at four o'clock."

"By the gazebo?"

"Perfect. But I have to go now. I'll see you later."

He exhaled a breath he hadn't realized he'd been holding. This was definitely a step in the right direction. All he needed was the chance to make it right, and this boded well.

He'd taken some orange juice out of the refrigerator and was pouring it into a glass when his phone rang again.

Grabbing it with his free hand and still pouring with the other, he glanced at the caller ID, but it came up *number unknown*. Sometimes calls from the hospital registered like that. Since he wasn't on call this weekend, he wondered if it might not be Anna calling back from a landline to say she'd changed her mind about running this afternoon.

He pressed the talk button and held the receiver up to his ear. "You'd better not be calling to beg off."

Silence stretched over the line. After a moment, he almost hung up because it seemed as if no one was there.

"Yes, good morning. I'm trying to reach Jake Lennox." The voice was male, decidedly not Anna's.

"This is he," Jake said.

"Hello, Jake. It's Roger James. I hope I'm not calling too early."

Roger was Jake's landlord. The man and his wife lived in Florida. Since Jake paid his rent on time, he rarely heard from the home owner.

"Good morning, Roger. How are you?"

The two men made small talk for a few minutes—about Jake's career, about Roger and his wife June's plans to travel in the years ahead.

"Which brings me to my reason for calling," Roger said. "June and I are excited about our cruise and one of the things we're most excited about is streamlining our responsibilities. We wanted you to be the first to know that we're planning on putting the house you're living in on the market. Since you've been such a great tenant for so long, we wanted to offer you first right of refusal. Are you interested in buying the house? Since you've lived there for so long, seems like you might be ready to make that commitment now."

The park was crowded for a Sunday afternoon. Jake passed joggers and mothers pushing small children in strollers as he made his way across the grassy area to meet Anna. The weather was perfect, one of those cloudless robin's-egg-blue-sky days that should've had him feeling a lot better than he was when he finally spied Anna near the gazebo.

She was dressed in running shorts and a pink tank top that hugged those curves that were so fresh in his memory. Her hair was knotted up on top of her head and her long legs looked lean, strong and tanned as she did her prerun warm-ups.

He remembered how those legs felt wrapped around him and his body responded.

"Anna," he said, falling into sync with her as she performed lateral lunges to warm up her glutes. He did his best not to think about her glutes, and especially tried not to think about how his hands had been all over them as he pulled her body into his.

"Hey." She virtually pulsed with tension. Was that anxiety tightening her lips? He ached to touch her and had this mad vision of kissing her until she relaxed, but he knew that would only make things worse. So he kept a respectful distance. And tried his best not to think about her glutes.

"How was work?" he asked.

"Good," she said, going into the next sequence of stretches. Her movements were sharp and fast. Normally, she would've waited for him to start, maybe even stopped stretching to talk to him for a couple of minutes, but today she didn't.

And she was giving him one-word answers. Had he missed something here? Was she mad at him?

"Thanks for making time to get together," he said, immediately hating how he sounded so stiff and formal. For God's sake, this wasn't a business meeting. No, it was much more important. Thirty years of friendship was hanging in the balance here.

I mean, come on. We need to talk about this.

"Not a problem," she shrugged.

This was ridiculous.

"What's wrong?" he asked.

"Nothing," she said. "Just a long day…after a night rather short on sleep."

"If it makes you feel any better, I didn't get much sleep either."

"Why would that make me feel better?"

"Look, can we talk about this, please?"

"Jake, really, what is there to talk about?" she said.

He attempted a smile, but it didn't quite make it. As she brushed a strand of hair off her forehead, he saw her hand was trembling.

"Anna," he said. "Talk to me."

She took a deep breath. "Things got a little intense

last night." She shook her head. "You were vulnerable and I was so determined to help you feel better. I'm always trying to get you to open up." She lifted her shoulder, let it fall. "I guess I pushed it a little too far last night. Because you still won't let me in. I mean, there's the physical, and then there's letting me *in*."

She put her hand on her heart.

Jake shrugged, unsure what to say.

"Are you upset because I didn't spend the whole night with you?"

Apparently that was the wrong response, because she pinned him with a look that was almost a sneer, then turned away without answering.

"I wish letting you in were that simple. I mean, I'm not purposely keeping you at arm's length."

"Obviously not." She sat on the bench that was behind her and retied her shoe.

"Okay, so maybe we did get a little carried away last night. But when all is said and done, you don't want me, Anna. I'm not the man for you. You deserve so much more than I can give you."

"You already said that, Jake. I told you I disagree."

Wait. What was she saying? Did she think he was the man for her?

She turned and with a quick jerk of her head, she motioned for them to start their run.

Hell, he should've known this was going to happen. He was such an idiot.

"You said what we did, what happened between you and me, mattered to you, too. It does matter. I can't be *that girl*, Jake. The one who has casual sex with you and then goes out with someone else the next night."

"Anna, I know that—"

"Just, please let me talk," she said. Her voice was barely a whisper.

Jake went silent, waiting patiently, watching her.

Emotions seemed to be getting the best of her. Jake reached over and took her hand, but she pulled away, balled her hand into a fist and quickened her pace.

"Talk to me," he said softly. "It's me, Anna. It's still me."

"That's exactly what you said last night, and you're right—you are still *you*. I'd never expect you to change. You don't want to get married. Jake, I want a family someday. I know you don't. But I can't be your friend with benefits, hanging around and pretending we want the same thing."

"You may have noticed that I'm not the most experienced…woman in the world. I haven't been with a lot of men."

"Notice? Of course I didn't notice. You were great. Everything last night was great, except today you're upset and that kind of ruins everything."

She stopped running and stood there looking at him.

"You're only my second lover, Jake." She stared down at their hands. He was glad because he couldn't bear seeing the hurt in her eyes. He would never purposely hurt her for anything in the world. Not even for the best sex of his life— and what had happened between them last night was paramount.

If Hal had been her only other lover, she was a natural.

Or, Jake thought, maybe he and Anna were *that* good together.

God, he had to stop thinking like that. He'd caused her enough pain.

"You haven't had a lot of experience. It's not a big deal." He wanted to tell her that last night had taken him to places he'd never been, but he was afraid that would sound as if he wanted them to do it again. He wanted to. Damn, how he wanted to—he wanted to pull her into his arms right now and show her how much he wanted her and how good they were together—but then what?

All he had to do was look into her gorgeous blue eyes and he could see the hurt. He couldn't lead her down a dead-end path.

"You were married and faithful and that didn't give you a lot of opportunity for experience." *And some things simply came naturally.* "Plus, it's taken a while for you to get back on the dating path."

The dating path?

"Is that what this is?" she said dully. "The first step on the dating path?"

Her heart sank. She resumed jogging, hoping her inner anguish wasn't showing through in her eyes. Jake picked up the pace alongside her.

Of course this was the *dating path*. That's why Jake was fixing her up with his friends. If he was interested, he would've kept her for himself. He would've stayed the entire night rather than bolting like a stallion that had discovered a break in the fence.

After all, hadn't he told her before they'd crossed that line that he was still the same old Jake? He was who he was. She realized now what he probably meant was that making love wouldn't change him. It wasn't supposed to change anything. She'd promised him there would be no regrets and here she was on the verge of falling apart.

Get a hold of yourself, Anna.

Get a grip, girl.

Their relationship had been built on a solid foundation of friendship. She couldn't dig up that foundation now and replace it with a glass house. Because that's where a friends-with-benefits relationship would live, in a glass house that was likely to shatter as soon as one of them decided to slam the door.

In a split second that she saw the shattering glass in her mind's eye, she realized that even though she was sad, she needed to get a hold of herself and turn this around.

She had two choices: mope and lose, or cope and move on.

It wasn't hard to choose.

"You're right," she said. "It has taken me a while to get back on the dating path. I'm so glad you're okay with what happened between us and you won't let it change anything. No regrets, right? So, we're good, right?"

A look of relief washed over Jake's face and he reached out and squeezed her hand, holding it tighter than he should've. "That's exactly what I was hoping you would say."

Of course it was.

"Anna, you are amazing."

Of course she was. And if she told herself that, she might start to believe it. Because despite the cool-friend thing happening on the outside, on the inside the message that was echoing was, *He doesn't want you.* How had this gone so wrong? How had she not kept herself firmly planted in reality?

Somehow, she'd miscalculated. Somehow she'd misread the signs. She'd been turned on; he'd been vulnerable after the news about Bob. She'd been there, an easy refuge to temporarily unload his sorrows.

She imagined she could still feel the weight of his body on hers, feel the way he moved inside her.

"Okay, I'm glad we got that settled." Her voice was brisk. "I should get going, really."

"Anna? Are you okay?"

She was so pathetic that she thought for a moment she saw a flicker of worry flash in his eyes.

Well, Jake, you can't have it both ways.

But then it hit her; maybe it wasn't worry as much as it was pity.

Had it really come to this?

No. She wouldn't let it.

Jake Lennox might not be able to love her the way she wanted him to. But if it was the last thing she did, she'd make darn sure he didn't pity her.

"Of course. I told you. I'm fine. We're fine. No regrets."

She forced a smile, despite the fact that all she could think about was escaping to her house only a few blocks away. If she could get away from him and inside, she'd be okay.

"You don't look fine."

She conjured another smile. This one felt too big. "I told you I'm fine." *Liar, liar, pants on fire.* "I'm glad we're fine. But really, I need to go. I'm sure we both have things to do."

She knew she was smiling a little too widely and a very tiny part of her that she didn't want to acknowledge hoped Jake would see that she was so not okay, that she was drowning in it, actually. She'd fallen backward down a black hole that negated everything she wanted, and all that was left was this Cheshire cat smile and this need to run. God, she had to get out of there. Get somewhere she could think and make everything inside her feel right again. Because if she didn't, nothing in her world would be right.

Jake looked just as uncertain as she felt.

"Can I share something before we leave?"

Anna nodded.

"My landlord, Roger James, called me this morning. He's putting the house on the market. He gave me first right of refusal. What do you think about that?"

"What *I* think doesn't really matter," she said. "What do you think? Are you going to buy it? Plant roots?"

He shrugged and offered her a smile that wasn't really a smile.

"Who knows? Though I guess I need to figure it out pretty soon. Roger needs an answer soon. I've spent a lot of good years in that house. I've got my boat and a place to dock it. Where would everyone spend the Fourth of July?"

His smile was wistful.

"So what's the problem?" Anna asked. She hadn't meant to sound like such a witch.

"I haven't bought the place because I never intended to stay in Celebration. Not this long. But here I am. All these years have gone by…what am I doing?"

Anna felt her insides go soft. He was hurting and maybe she was being too hard on him. He'd lost a good friend, his home was being sold and last night they'd managed to jumble the only thing that made sense in either of their lives. She needed to cut him some slack, even if her own heart was breaking.

"Why are you always so hard on yourself? Look at all you've done. Not only do you have a good job, but you're in line for a promotion at the hospital. You're a valuable part of this community and you have friends who adore you."

She stopped short of saying, "And you have more women after you than you know what to do with." Clearly, he knew what to do with women.

"It's unexpected. I guess I just need some time to think about it. Buying a house is a big step."

"Maybe if you're eighteen."

Jake winced.

God, shut up, Anna. If you can't say something nice, don't say anything at all.

She bit her bottom lip to keep another snarky-sounding comment from slipping out.

"You're right. I'm thirty-four years old. I guess symbolically…buying this house feels like…" His voice trailed off and she gave him a couple of beats for him to finish the sentence, but he didn't.

So, she finished it for him. "Commitment?"

His eyes got large, like she'd just uttered the name "Bloody Mary" three times or spouted some other unmentionable.

"Touché," he finally answered.

Way to go, Anna. You made your point. Are you happy now?

She needed to leave so she could get herself together. Taking snipes at him, *especially* when he was clearly feeling bad about everything, wouldn't do anyone any good.

Besides, she'd been steering them toward her car, which was along the side of the park. Now they were there.

"Well, this is me," she said, pointing to her yellow VW Beetle. "I need to go. I have to be somewhere."

She clicked the key fob and heard the locks tumble. As if she didn't feel like enough of a heel for the way she was acting, Jake reached out and opened the car door for her. Why did he have to be nice when she was trying so hard to hate him right now?

Well, not *hate*. That wasn't the right word. She could never hate him.

In fact, what she was trying to feel was exactly the opposite…she was desperately trying not to fall in love with Jake Lennox.

"Thank you," she murmured as she slid behind the wheel.

He closed the door and she rolled down the window.

"I'm sure they don't need an answer tonight," she said. "Take some time to think about it. But, Jake, try not to overthink it. Just go with your gut."

He reached through the window and put his hand on her arm, snagging her gaze.

"You're right," he said. "I think we both need to stop overthinking things."

She watched him walk away. Damn him for being such a fine, fine man. And not just on the outside, but also inside.

She sat in the car for what felt like ages, long after Jake had disappeared from her line of sight, alternately feeling like an ogre and perfectly justified for pushing him away. This was exactly why friends didn't cross that line. It rendered things awkward and confusing. Despite how they'd promised each other that it would change nothing—that there would be no regrets—it had changed *everything*.

She needed to talk to someone who could help her put things into perspective.

She took her phone out of her glove box and texted her sister.

Need to talk to you.

Call me? Emily responded.

I'd rather talk in person.

Everything okay?

Anna didn't want to open the conversation over text. So, she answered with the only word that seemed to fit without going into detail.

Meh.

Is this about a guy?

Emily was so good at reading her.

Maybe.

I thought so. What are you waiting for? Get over here.

On my way.

Emily lived in an apartment just north of downtown. Anna arrived there in less than ten minutes and that was only because she hit every red light between the park and her sister's place.

When Emily answered the door she handed Anna a steaming mug of Earl Grey. Normally, Anna would've preferred iced water on a day like today, but hot tea was the sisters' ritual—just like she and Jake had the Sadness Intervention Dance.

Had was the operative word.

Anna's heart hurt at the thought of it. When they made each other sad, who was supposed to intervene with the dance now?

"Thanks, Em," she said as she accepted the mug and stepped inside. "What smells so good?"

"I'm baking cookies for tonight, but I think we need to do a taste test. There's oatmeal and chocolate chip."

"At least your apartment smells good. I'm sorry I don't. I just finished my run and wanted to come over before I went home to change to go to Mom and Dad's tonight."

"You don't smell bad, but just to be safe I'll hold my breath when I hug you."

Emily wrapped her arms around her sister. Anna was careful to not spill the tea. Then Emily took her sister's hand and pulled her toward her tiny kitchen. When Anna stepped inside, she could see a plate of deliciousness waiting for her atop her sister's glass-top café table.

"You're an angel, Em. This is exactly what I need."

Emily squinted at her sister, the concern obvious on her face. "What's going on?"

They sat down. Anna placed her cell phone on the table and took a sip of tea. It was supposed to fortify her, but instead it burned her tongue.

"I slept with Jake." As she blurted the confession, she set down the mug a little too hard. The table rattled and tea sloshed over the rim. Anna grabbed her phone to save it from the tea tidal wave and braced herself for her sister to call her a bull in a china closet or something equally as snarky. But when she looked up, Emily was staring at her wide-eyed and slack-jawed. She stumbled over her words for a moment, sputtering and spitting sounds that didn't form a coherent sentence.

"Oh! Uh. Well. Hmm. Ummm… Wow!"

Emily popped up and grabbed a paper towel and wiped up the spill with quick, efficient swipes. By the time she'd disposed of the soaked paper and returned to the table, she seemed to have collected herself. She smoothed her denim skirt and reclaimed her place at the table.

"I like that blouse on you," Anna said, suddenly feeling the need to backpedal. "You look good in magenta. I can't wear that color."

"Don't change the subject," Emily said. She gave her head a quick shake and a smile broke out over her pretty face. "This is the best thing I've heard in…maybe ever. Did I call it or what?"

"Stop gloating. It's not like that."

"Not like *what*?"

"It's not like however you're imagining it. Because if you knew how it really was, you wouldn't be smiling."

Emily's hand flew to her mouth. "No! Oh, no. Is Jake bad in bed?"

Anna squeezed her eyes shut for a moment, trying to block out the memory of exactly how far from the truth that was.

"No… Jake is actually quite good."

Emily's mouth formed a perfect O and her eyes sparkled. "*Ooh!* Do tell."

God, she couldn't believe she was talking about this. Even if it was Emily. She didn't kiss and tell…well, actually, with Hal there hadn't been much to talk about. So…

"Tell me everything," Emily insisted.

"I'm not going to give you a blow by blow—"

Emily snorted. She *actually* snorted.

Anna cringed when she realized her unfortunate choice of words. She couldn't help but think how gleeful Joe Gardner would've been if he'd heard that pun. He probably would've bowed down in reverence.

Anna frowned at her sister. "Are you thirteen years old? Get your mind out of the gutter."

"Well, this is a conversation about sex and according to you, it was mind-blowing. I'm not seeing the problem here."

Ah, the problem. Right.

Anna took a deep breath and, using very broad terms, she brought her sister up to date on the situation.

"I will not allow this to degenerate into a friends-with-benefits pseudo-relationship. But I'm so attracted to him, sometimes I can't seem to help myself. I knew exactly what I was doing last night, and I knew exactly how I would feel afterward, but I did it anyway. And I'm afraid I might do it again if I get the chance."

"Wow" was all that Emily could offer.

Anna plucked a chocolate chip cookie off the plate. It was still warm and gooey. Sort of like her resolve with Jake—unless she turned into the superwitch she'd been at the park.

"I'm mad at myself, but I'm taking it out on him. I mean, I know he feels bad because I'm acting like this and his good friend just died, and now *this*. What is wrong with me, Em? Was Hal right? Could he see all along that I was attracted to Jake? You saw something. Am I as much to blame for the breakup of my marriage as Hal was?"

And now she was babbling—because this wasn't about Hal. It was about Jake and her and how everything was now upside down.

"Don't be ridiculous," Emily said. "You weren't the one who cheated. I'm sorry to bring that up. But it's true. How can you be guilty of feelings you never knew you had. I mean…unless these feelings aren't new?"

"No! I promise you, this is as big a surprise to me as it is to you. Come on, this is *Jake*."

"Well, sis, I hate to break it to you, but Jake is pretty darn sexy."

"Tell me about it." Anna raked both hands through her hair and stared up at the ceiling.

"I am not going to play a game of 'Don't. Stop. Don't. Stop.' I just need to know how to get things back to where they were before. How do I do that, Em?"

The refrigerator motor hummed and, overhead, one of the fluorescent lightbulbs blinked a couple of times.

Emily sipped her tea, looking thoughtful. "First, if you're sure this relationship isn't good for you, you can't sleep with him again."

"I know that," Anna said. "I wish I could promise you I won't do it again."

"Hey, don't promise me. That's all on you. Personally, I think you two would make the perfect couple."

"Emily, stop. Jake and I want different things. He doesn't want to get married. He definitely doesn't want kids. I hate to admit this, but I'm not getting any younger. I do want kids. I never thought I'd be one of those women lamenting her biological clock. But here I am."

"God, you two would have gorgeous children."

"Emily. Have you heard a word I said?"

"Of course I have. But it's true."

Anna *tsk*ed. "*Really?* Are you going to torture me after I turned to you for help?"

Anna resumed her tea-gazing, and Emily reached out across the table and took her sister's hand.

"Even though it's my prerogative as your younger sister, I won't tease you. The next time you're alone with him, if you're afraid you're going to be tempted, text me an SOS and I'll come and rescue you."

"Actually, that's not a bad idea," Anna said. "The only thing is, unless I fix things with him, it's a moot point. I was so mean to him this afternoon, I'm ashamed of myself. I wouldn't blame him if he didn't want to talk to me. I don't even like me after the way I acted."

"Then that's all the more reason you need to talk to him," Emily said.

Anna grimaced.

"Don't be such a baby," Emily said. "Based on what you said, he was trying to meet you halfway this afternoon and you were a total B. You need to reach out and make this right. Tell him exactly what you told me. Except for the part about being in love with him."

Anna jerked ramrod straight in her chair. "I did *not* say that."

Emily tilted her head and smiled. "You didn't have to, sweetie. It's written all over you. You're oozing *Jake love* out of your pores."

Feeling her cheeks burn, Anna buried her face in her hands. "Am I that obvious?"

Emily nodded. "Sorry, hon, just calling it as I see it."

"Then I definitely can't…"

"You can't what?" Emily's voice sounded impatient in that way that only a sister could get away with.

"I can't call him. I certainly can't see him."

"So you're just going to let him walk away? You're essentially going to set a match to a thirty-year friendship and watch it burn? Is that what you want?"

"No." Even though the word came out as a whisper, Anna nearly choked on it.

"Then call him, for heaven's sake." With a manicured finger, Emily slid Anna's phone across the table. Anna recoiled and fisted her hands in her lap as if the cell would burn her if she touched it. "The longer you put it off, the more difficult it's going to be."

"I don't know what to say."

"Invite him to dinner tonight. You know Mom and Dad would love to see him. And Mom always cooks enough for fifteen. Think about it. A family dinner will take both of you back to your roots. How many times did he have Sunday dinner with us when we were kids? He was like a part of the family."

Hence the problem. Only he certainly didn't feel like a brother. Anna wondered if he ever had. She sighed. "Funny you mention it. I'd intended to invite him before everything got so weird."

"Then do it." Emily stood, pushing back her chair with the bend of her knees. The wrought iron scraped a mournful plea on the tiled kitchen floor. She picked up Anna's phone and handed it to her. "I'm going to go put in a load of laundry."

In other words, her sister was going to give her some privacy.

Once Emily cleared the room and before Anna could overthink it, she opened her phone address book to the

contacts that were saved as favorites—all six of them—
and pressed the button to call Jake's phone.

He picked up on the third ring.

"Hey, Jake, how about dinner tonight with the Adams
family?"

Chapter Ten

"Jake, honey, it's so good to see you," said Judy Adams. "It's been far too long."

"Thanks for letting me come to dinner tonight," he said, offering Anna's mom a smile.

"You have a standing invitation. Please don't wait for that daughter of mine to invite you."

Judy gave Anna a pointed look and Jake smiled at the way she blushed.

"Thank you," he said. "I appreciate that."

"Would you care for more lasagna?" Judy offered. "Hand your plate to Norm and he can dish it up for you."

"It's delicious, but I'm stuffed. In fact, everything was fabulous."

"I'm sorry we couldn't make it to the party yesterday," Norm said. "We'd promised my folks that we would take them to see the fireworks over in Plano. Now that they are in the retirement community, we have to get over there every chance we get."

Jake nodded. That was the thing about the Adams family; they seem to have longevity in their genes... and in relationships. Both sets of Anna's grandparents were still alive and together. This move to the retirement community for Norm's folks was a new turn of events. Earlier, Judy had mentioned that her parents were on a cruise around the world.

The Adamses' world was different from—in fact, it was polar opposite to—the one he'd grown up in. While the Adamses had always been generous to include him, more often than not he'd felt like an outsider looking in. That was all on him, though. It was nothing they'd done. They'd always been as warm and welcoming as they were this evening.

Jake glanced at Anna, who had been quiet for most of the dinner, allowing her sister to entertain with tales of crazy customers at the restaurant and a few sidebars about customer woes at the bank. As he listened to her talk, he wondered why his brother Luke had never shown an interest in Emily. The woman made no secret about her affinity for him. No doubt Luke had his reasons, and far be it from Jake to interfere.

Anna caught him staring at her. She gave him a shy smile and turned her attention back to the lasagna that she'd been pushing around on her plate. He'd been so glad to get her call. After the way they'd left things earlier in the park, he wasn't sure what to do next. He would've figured it out, because there was no way he was going to let this indiscretion come between them. He was simply going to give Anna some room until she was able to realize that, yeah, they may have feelings for each other—and there was nothing more that he wanted than to have her in his bed every night—but he wasn't the man for her.

The only conclusion he'd come to was he would make the ultimate sacrifice by putting a lid on his feelings for her to make sure that, eventually, she ended up with a man who deserved her.

They'd arrived at Judy and Norman Adams's place in separate cars. So they hadn't had a chance to talk. Yet here they sat in the same dining room, at the same table, in the same places that they'd occupied on all those Sundays all those years ago.

Judy and Norman each sat at each end of the table; Jake and Anna sat to Judy's right, Emily across the table from them. The dining room still had the same traditional feel and furniture set—a large table in the center of the room, a sideboard and china cabinet on opposite walls, blue-and-white wallpaper depicting old-fashioned scenes of men and women courting on benches and under trees. What did they call it? Tool or toile— something like that. It didn't matter.

What was important was that despite how everything had changed between him and Anna, there was still that connection, that lifeline that kept them from drowning. Sharing a meal with the Adamses felt as if they'd stepped back in time nearly a decade and a half. Suddenly, what he needed to do was as clear as the crystal goblet on the table.

He was going to let bygones be bygones and fix her up with Dylan Tyler. The guy had asked about Anna several times since he'd seen her at the jazz festival. Jake had had his trepidations about fixing up the two of them—if he was honest with himself, the feelings probably stemmed from his being afraid that Anna and Dylan might actually be a good fit. Not that he thought the dates he'd arranged for her wouldn't work, but it just took a few go-rounds to realize who would work—who would be the best person for her.

Jake mulled it over as he helped clear the table. That was one thing about the Adamses; they all pitched in and it made him feel even more like family when Judy and Norm didn't excuse him from doing his part—even after all these years.

During cleanup, he and Anna made small talk and, to the untrained eye, nobody probably realized anything was different. God, he hoped not. All he had to do to set himself straight was think of looking Norman Adams in the eye and telling him that he'd had a one-night stand with his daughter.

Yeah, that put everything into perspective.

When they finished washing the dishes, he said to Anna, "Want to take a walk around the old neighborhood?"

The unspoken message was "It's time we talked about this." He could tell by the look on her face she understood and that she was ready to talk.

Outside, twilight was settling over the old neighborhood. Fingers of golden light poked through the branches of the laurel oaks and the sun had painted the western sky with broad strokes of pink, orange and dusky blue.

It was always bittersweet coming and going from the Adams house. Because the house he'd grown up in was right next door. After leaving for college, Jake had only been back for Christmas and to visit his dad occasionally when he wasn't taking classes over the summer. When his dad had married Peggy—two years after Jake's mom had died—the house had gone from feeling discombobulated to cold and unwelcoming. Peggy, who was only twelve years older than Jake, had no interest in being a mother to Karen Lennox's children. The moment she moved in, it was apparent that the countdown clock had begun for when she could get the four boys out of *her* house and out from under the obligation of caring for them. At the time, Jake didn't realize what she was doing—even worse, he didn't realize that his father was allowing this woman to push his sons out of their own home. But that was because his father had always played the victim, making his wife out to be the villain who had walked out on her own family.

As Jake and Anna stepped out onto the sidewalk, Jake tried not to look too hard at the house next door to the Adams family. It looked cold and haunted and only dredged up the worst memories. As far as Jake knew, Peggy still lived there. He and his brothers hadn't had contact with her since the day of his father's funeral, when somehow Peggy had managed to let all four Lennox brothers know that she and their father had been together a lot longer than they had realized. They'd started seeing each other the year *before* his mother had left the family.

That was when everything had clicked into place. His mom hadn't just randomly left the family as his dad had led them to believe. She'd left because her husband was involved with another woman, and just a few days later she died in that accident, unable to defend herself or let her voice be heard—that she fully intended to come back for them once she was able to get herself established. Even though Jake had no hard evidence of this, he felt it down to his bones. It was so out of character for his mother to abandon her home and the children she adored. She had probably been flummoxed by the realization that the man she'd trusted with her heart was in love—or under the spell of—another woman.

The only good thing Peggy had ever done for Jake and his brothers was to tell them the truth, which had vindicated their mother. Of course, it had also revealed their father for the weak, henpecked, poor excuse of a man that he really was—letting Peggy dictate the fate of his family, turning a blind eye and simply going along for the ride because it was the path of least resistance.

If Jake had had trepidation about marriage and family before his father's death, Peggy's revelation was the wax that sealed the deal. Jake would never let himself be that influenced by a woman. After living with Peggy for years and seeing what she'd done to their father and family, Jake vowed never to let a woman render him weak like that.

As he turned his back on his childhood home and walked with Anna in the other direction, a warm evening breeze tempered the fierce July heat, making it almost pleasant to be outside. Still, Jake felt the heat of apprehension prickle the back of his neck because of what he was about to do. He just needed to figure out how to say it. He could go all corny and sentimental opening with the old saying, "If you love something, set it free." But that was a little dramatic. So he opted for taking the more direct route. But before he could find the words, Anna spoke.

"You might have wondered why I asked you here tonight."

He smiled because that was a line from some corny black-and-white television show that they'd been obsessed with one summer a long time ago.

"Actually, I think I have a pretty good idea. Anna—"

"No, let me go first. Please?"

He nodded. "Okay."

"I owe you an apology for how I acted this afternoon… and this morning."

"You don't have to apologize."

"Yes, I do. Because you don't deserve to be treated that way. No wonder you're afraid of commitment if women turn into needy, beastly creatures. Or am I the only one who acts like that? I'm so bad at this."

"Stop," Jake said. "You aren't being unreasonable. Don't ever compromise what's important to you. Okay?"

She nodded.

"Funny, how you and I had a better time with each other than any of the blind dates we've been on," Jake said after they'd cleared the Adamses' white colonial-style home. "But I've thought a lot about what you said, and you're right. You're not the kind of woman who sleeps with one guy and dates others."

Realizing that this preamble might sound as if he was going in a completely different direction than what he meant, he quickly added, "I would love to be with you, Anna. In fact, if I could create the perfect woman for me she would be someone just like you—"

"Only someone who didn't want the ultimate commitment, right?"

"I know that sounds ridiculous. Anyone of your caliber deserves everything she wants. I'm sorry, but I don't see myself ever getting married. That means no kids, which is probably a good thing, because if I got married and had a family, I'd probably screw up worse than my parents did."

Anna shook her head. "Are you really going to let your parents' mistakes steal the happiness of family from you? Isn't that just adding to tragedy on top of tragedy?"

"This is where you and I differ. We have completely different takes on what constitutes happiness. Family and happiness are not synonymous in my book."

"What about your brothers? You guys are pretty close. How can you say they don't bring you happiness?"

He thought about it for a moment. "My relationship with my brothers is so different it's hard to explain. Of course, I wouldn't trade them for anything in the world, but that relationship doesn't do anything to convince me that marriage is the right path for me. It's completely different. Anna, you have to remember that growing up I was more of a caregiver to my brothers, a parent rather than a sibling."

He was starting to feel hemmed in, cornered, having to defend himself. And that feeling made him want to run. But he couldn't. He and Anna needed to work through this. He had things to say to her, and he wasn't going to leave until those things were said and they were okay.

As he tried to cool his jets and regroup his thoughts, the question of what he might be capable of that would be worse than cheating and vilifying a dead spouse—the way his father had—niggled at the back of his brain. Of course, he didn't make a habit of lying and cheating. That's why he broke up with women when the relationship had run its course.

He glanced at Anna as they turned the corner off their childhood street. He did have a modicum of self-control. Except when it came to Anna, apparently. But Anna wanted both marriage and kids. As much as he wanted her—needed her—it wouldn't be fair to lead her down a dead-end path.

"There's still the bet," she said, sounding more like her old self. "Now that we've had a couple of warm-up rounds and we know the kinds of people who aren't right for us, maybe we should regroup and get going on that again. I'm going to win, you know."

Yes, thank you, that was his Anna. Her spirit had returned. Or at least she was trying. If he was completely truthful with himself, he wasn't convinced that Anna's too-broad smile was completely sincere. It called to mind those people who believed projecting the emotion that they wanted to feel would make it a reality—or something like that. But this was a start in the right direction.

"No, you're not. Because there's someone I want to fix you up with."

She groaned. "Who?"

"What do you think of Dylan Tyler?"

"The new doctor who works at Celebration Memorial?"

"The one and only."

"Dylan Tyler… Since the first time I heard his name, I wanted to ask, is he a good Southern boy with a double first name, or is that his first and last?"

"Very funny," Jake said.

Anna gave a one-shoulder shrug. "I don't know. He's handsome. I guess. I've not had the chance to get to know him."

"Now's your chance. I have it on very good authority that he would love to ask you out."

There was that too-wide smile again. It didn't match the dullness in her eyes.

"Oh. Goody."

"Wow. Your enthusiasm is overwhelming. Could you tone it down a bit?"

Anna shrugged again. "I don't know. You know how I feel about dating doctors. Do you think it's a good idea, since we work together? I mean, you saw how rumors flew when people thought you and I were…"

The same pink that had colored her cheeks earlier in the dining room was back. He knew exactly what she was thinking, and damned if his body didn't respond.

The primal, completely base part of his brain kicked in. God, if he didn't have good sense, he'd pull her into his arms right now and remind himself how much he wanted her.

But sparks faded and then you were left with real life.

What had happened between them was a cautionary tale, and if he really cared about her, he wouldn't lead her on.

Dylan Tyler called Anna the following day and asked her to be his date to the Holbrook wedding.

And she'd said yes.

Really, it wasn't as daunting as it seemed at face value. Given the circumstance, there would automatically be a barrier between them. The daughter of Celebration Memorial Hospital's CEO was getting married. Everyone would be on their best behavior.

Not that she expected Dylan to bring anything less.

This date felt safe. Like going to prom with the friend of a friend…even though her prom had happened more years ago than she cared to admit.

Tick…tick…tick…

Darn that biological clock.

Jake would be there.

Now she just needed to remind him that he'd agreed to ask Cassie Davis to be his date, and make sure he didn't revert to his old ways and ask someone like Miss Texas.

She hadn't given it much thought since they'd been otherwise occupied…with him being away at the conference…and them planning the Fourth of July party…and, well, everything else. But they needed to get back to their original plan. It was the only way to get their friendship back on track.

She jabbed the up button and tried to ignore the cold, hollow emptiness in the place where her heart should be. As she stood there, she tried not to think about how Jake had said his perfect woman would be someone like her. If she didn't know that he meant well and didn't believe that he would never purposely hurt her, she might think he was playing her.

Someone just like her, but not her.

Was that supposed to be a consolation prize? Because it sort of felt like a slap in the face.

She gave herself a mental shake.

Come on, Anna. You know the rules. It would be fruitless to try and change them.

Anna adjusted her grip on her insulated lunch bag, which contained a turkey sandwich on whole wheat with lettuce and tomato, an apple and some carrots. She had to go light since she had no idea whether or not she could fit into the cocktail dress she was going to wear to the wedding. It had been so long since she'd had a fancy occasion to wear it, she wasn't sure how it would fit. When she and Hal were married, it seemed as if there was something or another every other night, but the dates Jake had arranged had been informal and the dresses she'd purchased for them had been casual and not suitable for a wedding.

Funny, she hadn't missed the stuffy occasions at all. She didn't mind getting dressed up, but the so-called friends who really weren't friends at all… She didn't

even want to give them a second thought. She hoped
Hal's girlfriend was better suited to inane cocktail chit-
chat than she was.

You know what? On second thought, no. She didn't
hope she was better at it. She hoped the woman was
twice as miserable as she had been and that the so-
called friends made it even harder on the girlfriend
than they had on her.

Wow. That sounded really bitter.

She didn't want to be that way. Really, she didn't.
But after all she'd been through, couldn't she simply
get a break?

A little voice inside of her told her that maybe Dylan
was her break. Or at least a step in the right direction.
He was a good-looking guy. Light brown hair with sun-
streaks that looked natural. They'd better be. She re-
fused to date a man who spent more money on his hair
than she did. And if they were natural, at least that
meant that he liked to spend time outside. That was
one thing they'd have in common, besides working for
Celebration Memorial.

Anna wasn't prepared to list the fact that they were
coworkers in the pros column just yet. In fact, she was
very nervous about it. At least he worked on the second
floor and rarely, if ever, got up to the third floor, which
was why she hadn't had a chance to get to know him.

But Jake had handpicked Dylan for her. That had to
mean something, didn't it? Especially given the delicate
nature of their own relationship right now.

She decided she owed it to herself to approach it
with an open mind. She'd given Jake the advice that "if

you keep doing what you do, you'll keep getting what you get." Maybe she needed to borrow a page from her own book.

The elevator chimed and Anna waited for the people who'd ridden down to step out. Then she got in and pushed the button for the third floor. As the doors were closing, she heard a woman call, "Hold the elevator, please?"

With a quick jab of her finger, Anna managed to re-open the doors before the car lifted off.

As if fate had conjured her, Cassie Davis rushed inside, uttering a breathless "thank you so much. You know how slow these elevators are. If you hadn't waited for me, I'd be late. As it is I'm cutting it close."

"No problem," Anna said. "I'm glad I could help."

She was glad they weren't clock watchers up on three. Then again, she was usually early or right on time like she was today, but she understood how missing the elevator could cost you a solid five minutes, and it always happened at the most inopportune times.

"I guess I could've taken the stairs," Cassie said. "But given how my morning has started, I probably would've fallen on my face. I just hate being late."

"Me, too," Anna said, studying the woman with her pretty peaches-and-cream complexion, blue eyes and auburn hair. Yes, she would remind Jake that he'd agreed to take Cassie to the wedding. Cassie was perfect for him. Maybe even a little too perfect, but she couldn't think about that right now.

The elevator dinged to signal its arrival at the second floor.

"Cassie, I don't mean to be nosy, but are you dating anyone?"

The woman did a double take as she started to exit the elevator. Anna jabbed the door open button again to give Cassie time to answer.

"No. I'm not. Why do you ask?"

If it was possible to be simultaneously happy and disappointed, that was how Anna felt hearing the news. But of course she wasn't involved with anyone. She'd been practically drooling over Jake that day Anna had filled in on the second floor.

"Because I have someone I want to fix you up with."

Cassie smiled. "Oh? Do I know this person?"

"You do. It's Dr. Lennox. Are you interested?"

Cassie's jaw dropped for a moment. "Absolutely."

"Good. He's going to call you soon. Today probably. Can he find your number in the hospital personnel directory?"

"Yes."

"Good." She looked so happy and Anna tried to convince herself it was a good thing. It *was* a good thing. Jake would have an appropriate date for the wedding and Anna would…just have to be okay with that. At least she got to pick his date.

When the door started to close, Cassie reached out and stopped it. "I need to ask you a question, though." Her brows were knit. "I thought you and Dr. Lennox were involved."

Anna mustered her best smile. "Jake and I are good friends. He's like a brother to me."

Cassie looked even more confused. "Oh. Okay…?"

"I need to run. Neither of us wants to be late."

Anna waved and Cassie pulled her hand away. As the doors closed, she looked as if she were trying to decide whether Anna was playing a practical joke on her. Anna knew that because that was what she would've been wondering if the tables were turned.

Poor Cassie.

Actually, no. Not poor Cassie. Lucky Cassie.

Just don't fall in love, she wanted to warn Cassie.

The elevator chugged slowly up to the third floor and when the doors finally opened on the maternity ward, Anna's heart skipped a beat when she saw Jake standing at the nurses' station. His back was to her. But she'd recognize those shoulders anywhere.

She drew in a deep breath to steady herself.

"I didn't know you were pregnant," she said as she approached, trying to use humor to cover her own nerves. He turned around at the sound of her voice.

He ran a hand over his flat stomach. "Oh, am I showing?"

Anna laughed as she reached over the counter that defined the nurses' station and set her lunch bag, keys and phone on the desk.

"What are you doing up here in baby-land, Dr. Lennox? Are you lost?"

She spied the personnel directory, looked up Cassie Davis and wrote her name and phone number on a piece of note paper that was next to the computer.

"I just happened to be in the neighborhood."

"Is that so? Well, then, you are lost. Walk with me and I'll help you find your way."

Good grief, if there were a ship called *The Mixed Messenger*, Jake would've been the captain, because one minute he was making love to her, and the next he was fixing her up on a blind date. Before the fireworks on the Fourth of July, she wouldn't have thought twice about him dropping by like this…for no reason. Now she just needed to put what had happened out of her mind and remember how things used to be.

"Will you cover for me for a few minutes?" Anna asked Patty and Marissa.

"Sure thing," Patty said, looking up from the patient charts she'd been pretending to be engrossed in.

Anna could feel her coworkers watching her and Jake as they walked toward the elevator bank where they would have the most privacy, at least for the five minutes that it took the elevator to chug its way up to the third floor.

"Did Dylan call you?" he asked once they were out of earshot.

"He did."

"Good. And you two have a date?"

"We do. And so do you."

"No I don't."

"I'm fixing you up with Cassie Davis."

"I'm going out of town tomorrow. I'm going back to New Orleans for Bob's funeral."

"I'm sorry. I'm glad you're able to go, though."

The stress showed around his eyes. There was a tightness in his lips and in the way he held himself that had Anna wanting to give him a shoulder massage… and offer other means of stress relief—that she couldn't even believe she was thinking about, given where cross-ing that line had gotten them.

She blinked away the thought and held out the piece of paper with Cassie's number.

"Here, take this. She can be your date to the wedding this weekend. You will be back in time for the wedding, right?"

Jake nodded, but he looked as if he were about ready to balk at her suggestion to call Cassie. Anna preempted his protest.

"Look, you're the one who agreed to let me find you a date for the occasion. Cassie is nice. And appropri-ate. The chief knows her and will instantly realize that you have good taste in women. Besides, it's not like you have a lot of suitable options."

He took the paper and shoved it in his lab coat pocket.

"I know you have a lot of your mind, but will you call her before you leave for New Orleans?"

Jake shrugged, obviously not very enthusiastic about the date.

"I don't know that I really even need a date. I can just go to the ceremony and give my congratulations. It's not as if a date is mandatory."

"Yes, it is mandatory. You and I have a bet going on. If I'm going with Dylan, then you have to go with Cassie."

Technically, she knew he didn't have to do anything he didn't want to do. For that matter, he didn't have to go to the wedding either. But it was in his best interest to do so. And so was bringing a date like Cassie.

"You told me that you'd do anything to get things

back to normal between us. Taking Cassie to the Holbrook wedding will go a long way toward that end."

He shot her an incredulous look and she knew that he knew that she was making this up as she went along. But there was some substance to it. Because maybe if she saw him with another woman—a woman who was good for him, who might possess whatever it was that she lacked to change his mind about commitment—maybe they could get back to being just friends.

But what if he really fell for Cassie?

Didn't it always happen that way? A man swore he'd never get married, until the right woman came along and turned his entire belief system on its head. Whether or not Cassie was that woman, Anna hoped that seeing him with someone else would shock her own system enough to stop her from falling in love with Jake.

Because it seemed no matter how she tried to put on the brakes, her heart just kept careening toward disaster.

Chapter Eleven

Jake hated funerals.

Not that anyone loved them, but he'd developed a particular aversion since attending his mother's all those years ago.

Funerals weren't for the dead; they were for the living, a means to say goodbye, or maybe it was more apt to say that they were a reality check to make you aware that everyone's clock was ticking, that every day that you were fortunate enough to wake up and see the sun rise, you were also one day closer to death.

Funerals were a stark reminder to stop putting off the things you wanted to do and to handle everyone you loved with care, because death spared no one—it was the one thing that all humans had in common, Jake mused as he stood in sober contemplation and looked around.

The turnout at Bob Gibson's service was overwhelming. Standing room only.

Jake's plane had been delayed. By the time he'd arrived in the church and squeezed in among the latecomers standing along the back wall, one of Bob's sons, who looked to be about Jake's age, was already giving the eulogy.

"There are so many things in life that are uncertain, but love—unconditional love—is one of the few things you can invest in and get a return that far exceeds the outlay. My parents' marriage—the example they set—always had a profound effect on my life."

Lucky guy.

"Love isn't easy. In fact, by nature, it's complicated and messy, but without it, what do we have? A career? A fancy car? A big house? But what does it all mean without someone to share it?"

Jake's shirt collar was beginning to feel a little tight. He reached up and loosened his tie. The sun was streaming in through the stained-glass windows and the effect gave the sanctuary an otherworldly feel. A large portrait of Bob sat on an easel in front of the podium from which his son spoke. The way one shard of light hit the frame, it seemed to cast a halo over Bob's image.

Jake shifted his weight from one foot to the other, alternately looking at Bob's son, who looked a lot like him, and his friend's photo.

"I'm sure Mom won't mind me sharing that there were times in their marriage when the obstacles seemed nearly insurmountable, when both of them, in turn, had to sacrifice what each wanted for the other. But they always put each other's wants and needs ahead of their own. My parents rode out the storm when it got tough. My dad always told me you don't give up on the people who matter."

During Jake's internship, Bob had been more of a father figure to him than his own dad. Jake recalled a couple of times when Bob had to exercise some tough love, calling him on his own BS and giving him a reality check when he got too full of himself. Even though Jake didn't believe it at the time, it was now clear that his mentor's high expectations were one of the driving forces that saw him through the challenging years of becoming a doctor.

You don't give up on the people who matter.

How many times had Bob said that to him? More important, how many times had he demonstrated it?

The last time he saw Bob, they'd talked about marriage and family. Bob had seemed perplexed when Jake had told him he had no plans to get married. In fact, he'd urged him not to close his mind. And much like what his son was saying today, he'd warned Jake of the shallow trappings of succees. And also, he'd advised him to not let his career consume him because the body aged and success was a fickle mistress who didn't offer a whole lot of warmth in your golden years.

What does it all mean without someone to share it?

As the choir began singing "Amazing Grace," Bob's son returned to the church pew. He sat between his mother and a younger woman, who Jake guessed was his wife. He put an arm around each of them. Something in that protective gesture—or maybe it was the picture of his mentor bathed in that holy light—evoked a feeling that was strange and foreign.

Just last week Bob had been so alive. And now he was gone.

Something shifted inside Jake.

Feeling a little light-headed, he tugged at his collar again. It was just the heat—and possibly the prospect of ending up alone…or even worse, dying without allowing himself to love.

The rest of the week went by in a blur. Even though he'd only taken off one day, Thursday, flying to New Orleans and back on the same day, he just couldn't seem to get everything back in sync when he got to work on Friday.

To compound matters, he also realized on Friday morning he hadn't called Cassie to ask her to the wedding. He only remembered when she said hello to him as he passed the second-floor nurses' station.

He was surprised that Anna hadn't been on his case about it. But what was almost more disconcerting was when he realized how little he'd seen of her this week.

He paused in front of Cassie, not quite sure what to say, uncertain if it would be insulting to ask her to a big event the day before it happened or—"Hi, Cassie."

It was one of those rare moments when they were the only two at what was usually a hub of activity.

He figured he might as well ask. She could always say no and call him a cad for waiting until the last minute. If he ended up going to the wedding stag, at least he could tell Anna that he'd tried.

Cassie was cute, he supposed. Auburn hair—similar to Anna's—with large, sparkling blue eyes that seemed to light up when he stopped in front of her. He hated to admit it, but even though they worked on the same floor, he'd never really noticed her unless she spoke first. Not that he meant to be rude or disrespectful, but he was usually so focused on patients and their charts that sometimes he navigated the hospital on autopilot.

"Hey, so," he said, stumbling over his words, "I'm sorry this is such late notice. I meant to ask you earlier. Actually, I meant to call you, but I— Anna gave me your number. You know Anna Adams, right?"

Cassie smiled at him enthusiastically as she bobbed her head. "Right, she mentioned that she would like to give you my number."

Wait. Should he be doing this here? The hospital didn't have a no-fraternizing policy. So officially, he wasn't breaking a rule. But something just didn't feel right.

"I'd love to get together sometime," Cassie offered, seeming to sense his hesitation.

"Good. Are you free tomorrow night? Stan Holbrook's daughter is getting married and I, uh, RSVP'd for a plus-one."

Wow, that sounded enticing.

But it didn't seem to dull Cassie's shine. "That sounds lovely."

She jotted something on a piece of paper and handed it to him. "This is my address. I wrote my phone number down in case you need it. What time should I be ready?"

* * *

The next day, Jake had picked Cassie up at five-thirty for the six-thirty wedding. Even though she looked lovely, he couldn't seem to take his eyes off Anna, whom he'd picked out in the crowd in the hotel ballroom. She was with Dylan, of course. They were sitting two rows ahead of where he and Cassie were seated. Upon seeing them together, Jake instantly regretted setting them up.

What was wrong with him? He couldn't stand the thought of being tied down, but he hated the thought of her with someone else. The thought of Dylan possibly putting his hands on her the way he had the night they were together had him fisting his hands in his lap as they waited for the bridesmaids to finish parading down the aisle.

Cassie reached out and touched his hand. "You okay?"

Jake relaxed his hands. "Yeah," he whispered. "Fine."

Of course, that was the moment Anna made eye contact with him and smiled.

"She looks beautiful, doesn't she?" Cassie said.

Was he that obvious? Apparently so, since most of the guests were turned in their seats watching the bridal party parade, but Jake was facing forward, staring at Anna.

He was relieved when Stan Holbrook and his daughter finally appeared and everyone stood up and gave the bride their attention. Even Cassie stopped asking him questions and stood silently as the bride floated by.

What had happened to him over this past month since Anna had been back? She was Anna, through and through, but she was different, too. Or at least he was different.

In the good old days, the one thing Jake disliked almost as much as a funeral was a wedding, but tonight as he listened to this man and woman that he didn't even know exchange their vows and promise to love and honor and cherish each other until death did them part, something similar to what he'd experienced at Bob's funeral stirred inside him again.

What does it all mean without someone to share it?

Jake wished he knew the answer to the question, because it seemed as if it held the key to eternal happiness… or a life sentence without it.

After the ceremony was over, he lost sight of Anna as the guests filed out of the ballroom into another lavishly decorated room that was twice the size of the first.

A server with a tray of champagne stopped in front of them.

"Would you like something to drink?" Jake asked.

"Yes, thank you."

When he only took one flute off the tray, Cassie asked, "Don't you like champagne?"

"Oh, I forgot to mention I'm on call tonight. So I can't drink. It's your lucky night. I'm your designated driver."

Cassie lifted her glass to Jake and sipped the golden liquid.

It was in that moment of brief silence that Jake spied Anna and Dylan across the room. They were just entering the ballroom. Dylan had his hand on the small of Anna's back, causing the same possessive force that had driven Jake to fist his hands to consume him again.

"When did Anna start dating Dr. Tyler?" Cassie asked.

"They're not dating." Jake realized his tone might have been a little brusque.

"Well, that's good for you. Isn't it?"

"Why would you say that?"

Cassie cocked her head to the side and smiled up at him. "It's pretty obvious that you have a thing for her."

Oh, hell.

"So, is it that obvious?"

"Pretty much," she said with a sweet smile.

Out of respect, Jake did his best to avoid looking at Anna—since he was that obvious. One of the great things about Cassie Davis was that she was exceedingly easy to talk to. She was great at making conversation. As the various courses of the dinner were served, they not only made lively conversation with the other guests at their table—some of whom they knew from the hospital—but they also talked to each other about neutral subjects, like recent happenings at the hospital and the food they were served for dinner, such as the merits of the steak versus the salmon. She was funny and quick-witted and quite enjoyable, but there was absolutely zero chemistry between them.

Cassie was the kind of woman who would be fun to hang out with, but she was definitely 100 percent in the friend zone, and he had a feeling the feeling was mutual. She shared a lot of the same qualities that he found so attractive in Anna—they were both nurses, they both had a similarly unpretentious way about them that cut through the nonsense and went straight to the heart of the matter. Cassie was also fun to dance with when the music started and an all-around nice person, but that was as far as it went.

As the night went on, it became clear that Anna was either otherwise occupied or avoiding him, too. Because other than the smile that they exchanged before the ceremony, they hadn't had any contact.

And then the unthinkable happened. The wedding band decided to change things up. The singer said, "This one is by special request." The band broke into the first strains of "Don't Worry, Be Happy."

Immediately, his gaze snagged Anna's across the ballroom. He wasn't so sure it was an appropriate request to make at a wedding, but he was glad Anna had done it. Of all the icebreakers—well, aside from taking Cassie to the wedding at Anna's insistence—Jake hadn't been able to think of any that would get them back to the other side of the line that they had crossed. It had actually started to feel like a futile battle—a one-man war with himself.

What does it all mean without someone to share it? Don't worry. Be happy.

Cassie must've noticed, because she said, "Go ask her to dance. You can't ignore her all night. Good grief, I think I need to be your romance coach. And I mean that in the most platonic way possible, just in case there was any question. But somehow I don't think so. Go dance with her and then I need to think about leaving. I have to be at work early tomorrow."

* * *

"I can't believe you requested this song," Anna said once she was on the dance floor with Jake.

"Don't Worry, Be Happy" was one of those songs that was too slow to fast-dance to, but too fast to slow-dance to. So they did a modified version of the swing dance where Jake alternately sent her spinning out in turns and pulling her back in close.

"I didn't request it," he said as he reeled her back in and held her for a moment. "I thought you did."

Anna pulled back and looked at him. "Are you kidding? The guy in the band said someone requested it."

"I wish I had," Jake said. "Looks like fate intervened and requested for us."

"I guess so. How was New Orleans? I haven't had a chance to talk to you since you got back."

He looked so handsome in his suit and tie. The deep charcoal of the merino wool fabric echoed his dark hair and offset his blue eyes in a way that made her a little breathless. Good thing she could blame it on the dancing.

"It was a quick trip, and you know how I feel about funerals—"

"Yeah, the same way you feel about weddings."

He arched a brow and nodded solemnly. He really was taking Bob's death harder than she'd realized. She had the urge to pull him in close and hug him until all the anguish melted away.

But she knew better than that.

"Looks like you and Cassie are getting along well," Anna said.

This time when he reeled her in, he pulled her in close, slipped his right arm around her waist and held her left hand, guiding her to a slow sway. Her curves molded to the contours of his lean body, making her recall what had happened a week ago tonight.

"Cassie's a lot of fun," he said.

If Anna didn't know better, she might've thought the muddy feeling that washed over her was her heart sinking. But she was happy for her friend; really, she was. She wanted Jake to meet someone who could take his mind off all the ick that had happened lately. Someone who was just in it for the fun. He really was due for an upswing, and Cassie sounded perfect.

"Does that mean there's going to be a second date?"

He stared down into her eyes and she felt the connection all the way down to her soul.

"No, I don't think Cassie and I are suited to date. But we should definitely put her on the list to invite her to the Fourth of July party next year."

Oh. She knew she shouldn't read too much into that comment. He was just making conversation, not future plans. A lot could change in a year. He could meet the woman of his dreams. She could meet…someone.

"I'll make a point of adding her to the guest list."

She could feel the warmth of his hand on the small of her back, and for a moment she lost herself in the feel of it. Even though other people had joined them on the dance floor, for a moment it was just them. And it was so nice.

"So, how about you and Dr. Tyler? You are looking pretty cozy over there."

"Cozy? I wouldn't call it that. He's nice."

Jake's eyes widened. "You're perfect for each other. He's a great guy, Anna. Really, he is. I'm happy for you. I'm sensing that I'm getting closer to winning the bet?"

"You're getting a little ahead of yourself there, bucko. It's kind of hard to get to know a person at a function like this. It almost feels more like going through the motions with a rent-a-date—or maybe *arrange-a-date* is a better way to put it. In fact, maybe you should consider that before you write off Cassie. Keep an open mind."

Jake had a funny look on his face. Maybe he was considering Cassie in a different light.

"What are you thinking about?" she asked.

He was gazing at her so intensely, it was obvious that he wanted to say something—

"What, Jake?"

Their song ended and the band started a set of Southern rock 'n' roll, but Jake didn't move his hands and Anna stayed in his semi-embrace.

"Bob's funeral had a stronger impact on me than I realized. Life is short and there's no time to waste. It hit me like a train."

Wow. This was news. Where was he going with it?

She had to lean in closer because the music was so loud. She could smell his aftershave and that heady mix of sexy that was uniquely Jake. For a fleeting moment, she thought she could stay right here, breathing him in the rest of her life. But then there was a cold hand on her shoulder—a hand that wasn't Jake's—and it made her jump.

"Hey, guys," said Dylan. "Mind if I cut in and dance with my date, buddy?"

No. She wanted to hear what Jake had to say. But the moment was over, ruined. It was probably way too noisy to have that conversation now anyway.

"Sure thing, buddy," Jake said, stepping away from Anna and extending his hand for Dylan to shake. Dylan gave Jake's hand a hearty pump.

Ahh, the international man-sign for *I hear you, I see you; no harm, no foul.*

"Cassie and I need to leave anyhow. She has to work early in the morning and I'm on call. You know what it's like to be the only sober man at a rollicking party."

He winked at Anna.

"Hey," she said before he turned to walk away.

"But they haven't even cut the cake yet," she said.

"Have a piece for me, okay?"

Dylan put his hand on her shoulder, and she had to fight the urge to take a step away from him to reclaim her personal space.

"Call me later so you can finish telling me what you were saying about Bob's funeral. It sounds important."

There was that intense look again. It had her stomach flipping all over again.

"Okay," he said. "Don't you kids stay out too late. Anna, we will talk later."

Chapter Twelve

Anna was surprised when Jake's text came through. She didn't think he'd contact her since it was after ten o'clock, much less ask if he could come over.

Dylan had dropped her off about fifteen minutes ago and she was glad she hadn't immediately changed out of her cocktail dress and scrubbed her face free of makeup. All that she'd had time to do was kick off her shoes, take down her hair and brew herself a cup of tea.

After she'd texted Jake back, she remembered he was on call. So she added some water to the kettle so she could offer him a mug of something nonalcoholic when he arrived.

As she bobbed her own tea bag up and down, more for something to do with her nervous energy rather than to hurry up the tea, she couldn't help but wonder what was so urgent that he needed to talk to her tonight.

Unless he'd been worried about Dylan putting the heavy pressure on her and was dropping by to make sure she was in for the night, safe and sound. Dr. Tyler had tried to make a campaign for a nightcap, but Anna had nipped that in the bud right away. And to Dylan's credit, he hadn't pushed. Although he had told her he'd like to see her again. That was the part of dating that never got any easier—how did you let someone down easy and tell them you just weren't feeling it?

He was a great guy. Any woman in her right mind would be thrilled to spend an evening with him. He was good-looking—even if he wasn't her type. But why wasn't he? He was handsome, successful and funny. He didn't chew with his mouth open. Yet that indefinable *je ne sais quoi* was missing, and no matter how Anna tried to concentrate on the good, all she could think about was that she just wasn't that into him.

He wasn't Jake.

Damn you, Jake Lennox. Have you ruined me for all men?

If Anna could've slapped herself, she would've. She was sitting here pouting like a petulant child who was moping because she didn't get exactly what she wanted.

Buck up, buttercup. You don't always get what you want.

Sadly, she couldn't even convince herself that Dr. Tyler might be what she needed if she just gave it time.

No, what she needed was to be on her own for a while. This dating bet with Jake had started out as fun, but suddenly it had turned so serious. And that wasn't fun.

Or maybe what wasn't fun was the possibility of Jake changing his mind about Cassie. It had dawned on her that maybe he could tell how down she was at the wedding and didn't want to completely ruin her night with the confession that he actually was feeling it with Cassie.

Okay, now she was just assessing.

But just to be safe, maybe she should fix Cassie up with Dylan. They'd make a good couple.

Anna had gathered the flowers from the Fourth of July centerpieces and put them in a large vase, which sat in the middle of her kitchen table. The flowers caught her eye and took her back to that night one week ago. It hadn't been too much later than it was right now when things began to heat up with Jake.

Anna's heartbeat kicked up as she remembered the way he'd leaned in and kissed her on the dock, pulling her onto his lap and then coming back to her house to finish what he'd started.

Her breath hitched in her chest. What if that was why he was coming here tonight? He might not even realize that was what he was doing.

And that was exactly how things *just happened* between two people who knew better, who swore that they wouldn't fall into that friends-with-benefits trap. They started dropping in for late-night visits and—*Oh! Oops! Gosh, I didn't mean for that to happen…* And pretty soon they'd established a pattern of *Oh! Oops!*

Gosh! I promise it'll never happen again…after this one last time.

And damn her all to hell. She wasn't going to call him and tell him not to come over.

For a split second—actually, it was more like a good several minutes, a fantastic several minutes—she played out her own *Oh! Oops! Gosh!* production in her head.

What was she doing? The only thing that might be worse than having slept with Jake was to continue sleeping with Jake, knowing full good and well how he felt. He was her drug, and she needed to go cold turkey if she had any self-respect at all. Good grief, this wasn't only about that; it was about self-preservation.

She grabbed her phone and pulled up Emily's number. Before she could change her mind, she texted, SOS! It's urgent! Need you to come over now and save me.

She'd just pushed the send button when Jake knocked at the door.

So, he was still choosing to knock and wait, rather than doing their special knock and walking in the way he always had in the past. Then again, it was pretty late. She had locked her door behind Dylan, not that he would come walking in uninvited, but it just felt like an extra barrier between her and her date and the night.

And now Jake was here.

She padded to the door in her bare feet and looked out the peephole. There he was—all six foot four of him, with his perfect hair and perfect face and those perfect arms that had held her so close she didn't know where her body ended and his began.

Oh, dear God, Emily, please get here as soon as you can.

As she unlocked the dead bolt and pulled open the door, it dawned on her that she and Emily had never seriously talked about the SOS call. In fact, they'd sort of joked about it. Emily was probably working tonight. Of course she was on Saturday night.

Oh, crap.

Oh, well… Maybe she should ask for a sign from fate. Toss it up to the heavens. If she should sleep with Jake just one more time, Emily would *not* show up. If it was a bad idea, her sister would come to her rescue.

In the kitchen, the teakettle whistled, as if calling her on her BS.

I know, I'm a weak, weak woman. So shoot me.

Well, she would probably want to be put out of her misery if she let it happen again… But others had died for much less.

"Good evening, Dr. Lennox. Won't you come in?"

That was corny, she thought as she stepped back to allow him inside. Oh, well, that was what they did sometimes. That was why they were so darn good together—

But Jake wasn't moving. His feet were planted firmly on the front porch, and Anna was sobered by his stiff demeanor. He didn't look like a man who'd come to seduce a woman who would be oh-so-easy to take.

Oh, God! He's going to marry Cassie.

Anna actually took a step forward and looked out on the porch to see if maybe Cassie was waiting there to deliver the happy news with him. But no, he was alone.

"Are you going to come in? Or are you going to stand there and let the mosquitoes in?"

Jake flinched. "Sorry."

He moved inside like a man on autopilot—or maybe someone who wasn't feeling well.

She shut the door behind him and turned the lock. "Are you okay?"

"No, not really—" He made a face. "What's that noise?"

"Oh! It's the teakettle. I put on some water to make you a cup of tea since you're on call tonight."

Anna hurried back to the kitchen to stop the racket.

"What kind of tea would you like? I have English Breakfast, Earl Grey and peppermint. The peppermint is caffeine-free, but the bergamot in the Earl Grey supposedly has properties that will lift your spirits."

"I don't care," he called from the other room. "Whatever you have handy."

She glanced at her phone, which was lying on the kitchen counter, to see if Emily had responded. Nothing. Not a single word in response to her SOS.

Hmm. Okay, then.

They'd have a cup of tea—she opened a package of Earl Grey, just in case Jake needed the caffeine—and see where fate led them.

Anna carried the two mugs of tea into the family room, set them on the trunk that she used as her coffee table, and took a seat on the couch next to Jake, leaving just enough room to be respectable, but not enough room to send the keep-your-hands-off-me signal.

Careful, Anna...

Oh, shut up. Loosen up. Maybe Jake was right; maybe she needed to stop overthinking things.

"Is this about the house?" *Of course it wasn't. Although she was curious and it was a neutral subject.* "Have you made a decision about whether or not you're going to buy it? I love that house. I can't imagine you living anywhere else."

"Good, because Roger accepted my offer today."

"Jake, that's fabulous news. I'm so happy for you." She threw her arms around him and it felt so right. "And selfishly, I'm glad because that means you're staying put. Because I can't imagine being that far away from you again."

He pulled back slightly and looked at her. For a heart-rending moment, she couldn't read him.

God, had she said the wrong thing?

"I mean…since I just moved back. And all."

He was just frozen. Looking at her. She'd always known what he was thinking. Sometimes better than she'd known her own mind. But now…? Not so much.

"What's going on, Jake? I'm worried about you."

"Don't be," he said. "Or maybe you should be. Because I don't know what's happening to me. One minute, I was so sure where my life was going and what I wanted and what I didn't want. The next, everything was different. I just started seeing my life from a whole new perspective."

Uh-oh. Maybe this is about Cassie.

They had looked awfully cozy at the wedding, talking and laughing.

Oh, my God. He is here to break the news to me

gently. Of course, it wasn't as if Cassie was a complete stranger. Not even really a blind date. They worked together. He'd said it himself, he wanted someone like Anna, but not Anna… Jake was getting ready to settle back into another stretch of monogamy. Only it was with Cassie, and if anybody had the potential to move mountains and change his mind, she was the woman. And Anna had insisted they go out.

Oh, what have I done?

Jake scrubbed his face with his hands and gave his head a quick shake. "I'm sorry I came barging in here so late, and I start right in with what's on my mind and I didn't even ask you how things turned out with Dylan."

"That doesn't matter. I need to know what's going on with you."

Her heart was hammering so fast and loud that she was afraid he could hear it.

"Well, I can't say anything else until I know how everything went with Dylan. I need to know—are you going to see him again? It's important, Anna. Because whether or not you are could have a direct bearing on what I'm about to say."

Why? "What difference does it make?"

The look on Jake's face was so serious, she decided to quit playing games.

"He's fine. He's nice. I guess. A little possessive for my taste. Ha! I feel like I'm channeling you."

Then, the strangest thing happened. Jake was smiling at her in a way that made her lose her breath and she knew, she just knew that he was going to lean in and—

But at the sound of the front door opening, he flinched and diverted his lean toward his tea.

What?

Emily bounded into the room. "I got here as soon as I could."

Maybe it was because of Emily's abrupt entrance or maybe it was because she was giving him the look of death as she all but escorted him out, saying that she and Anna were having a girls' night and no guys were invited.

For the second time that night, Anna did not get to hear what Jake needed to tell her and seemed to be having so much trouble saying.

Damn her sister.

Damn that SOS text. Why had she been such a chicken, when in the end all she wanted to do was make love to Jake?

She'd followed him out to the porch, trying to ignore the fact that Emily was lurking in the living room. Anna had reached out and shut the door, putting a barrier between them and Emily.

"Jake? What were you going to say?"

Jake glanced back at the door and then at Anna. "Not now. Go back inside with Emily and I'll talk to you tomorrow."

Then his phone rang.

"It's the hospital. I need to take this. I'll talk to you later."

Rather than leaning in to kiss her, as she was so sure

he was going to do before Emily arrived, he picked up the call, saying good-night with a distracted wave.

She'd asked for a sign from fate and if this wasn't as clear as crystal, she didn't know what was. Still, all day Sunday, she waited for Jake to call as he'd said he would. She didn't want to call him since she wasn't sure how late he had been at the hospital dealing with the emergency.

Finally, at a quarter past two, she got a text. From Jake.

I know this is short notice, but are you busy tonight?

Defying common sense and her better judgment, Anna's heart leaped.

She didn't even wait a respectable amount of time to text him back. She grabbed her phone and typed, No plans, why?

Good. I've made arrangements for you to have one last date. I'm sure this guy is the one.

What? Was he kidding? He had nearly kissed her last night and now he was fixing her up on another blind date?

She typed, Sorry, I don't think so. I'm just not up for it.

How humiliating. Obviously, he was trying to pawn her off on someone to get her off his case.

She started typing again, Look, Jake, you don't need

to pair me up with someone to get me off your case. I get it. I understand.

As she hit Send on the second message, a message from Jake came through.

Please, just do this for me? This is the last date. I promise. I will never try to fix you up with anyone else again after tonight.

Oh, for the love of God. Was he really doing this?

She was about to type No and then turn off her phone. Instead, she opted for the path of least resistance.

I will meet him for a cup of coffee and that's it. And I'm driving myself. Then I'm off the hook. And just so you know, in case he doesn't want to waste his time, I'm giving him fifteen minutes max. And the clock will start the minute I walk in the door.

She probably sounded like a major B about it, but this hurt. And Jake was clueless. Or maybe he wasn't. Maybe he knew exactly what he was doing. If he'd come over last night to disengage, this date from out of the blue had completed the job for him.

A couple of moments later, Jake texted back, Actually, he has a seven o'clock reservation at Bistro St. Germaine. I guess you could have coffee in the bar. So, maybe get there a little early so they can give away the reservation if you really don't want to have dinner with him.

Really? Bistro St. Germaine?

She texted Emily, Are you working tonight?

But Emily didn't respond. She was probably tired of coming to her sister's rescue. Especially since, after Emily had scared Jake away last night, Anna hadn't been very gracious.

Anna had been in such a snit that Emily had opted for going home about half an hour later, once she knew that Jake was at the hospital and there was no risk of him coming back.

In fact, since he was going to such great lengths to pair her up with somebody—anybody, it seemed— it was pretty darn clear that there was no risk of him coming back at all.

It was just as well. She would give him space and maybe in a little while they could figure out how to be *them* again.

Even so, in that half hour last night, Anna had endured her sister's lecture of why she should avoid guys who didn't want to commit.

Hello? Wasn't that why she'd called in the first place? But she just let Emily say her piece.

It was just as well that her sister didn't return her text now.

To clear her head, Anna decided to go for a run. With each step, with each pounding of the pavement, she took out her frustrations and let off steam. Until she'd worn herself out, until she was so numb she felt nothing.

As she dragged herself back home, exhausted and emotionally spent, she vowed to take care of herself for a change. She'd spent so many years contorting and con- figuring her life to appease Hal, and in the time she'd been home, she'd let herself fall for another man who didn't want the same things she did—

She stopped herself.

Really, Jake hadn't done anything wrong. He hadn't lied or cheated. He may have led her on a bit, but she'd gone willingly, knowing what he wanted didn't align with what she wanted. So really, if anyone should shoulder the blame in that regard, it was Anna.

But that was where she was going to take care of herself.

She wasn't going to beat herself up.

Facts were facts: she and Jake were magnetically attracted to each other, but it simply wouldn't work.

End of story.

Around five-thirty, Anna freshened up, and prepared to make herself presentable. She washed her hair and blew it dry.

She kept her makeup very light, because she didn't wear much anyway.

Then she surveyed her closet and decided on a cute little shift with a bold blue and white print. It seemed brighter and happier than she felt.

The run had helped her let go of some of the sting of Jake's rejection-disguised-as-a-fix-up. It still hurt, but it had subsided to a dull ache. By that time, she'd decided she couldn't take it out on the guy who was meeting her tonight. Sure, she was only going to give him fifteen minutes, but she wasn't going to be rude or mean or vent her frustrations to him. After all, his only sin was that he wanted to meet her.

She would let him know that while she appreciated

his interest, this meeting had been a mistake. It wasn't a good time. She simply wasn't available right now. Not when her heart belonged to another.

A man who couldn't return her feelings.

When she got to Bistro St. Germaine, there was a space open on Main Street in front of the restaurant. It must have been her lucky day.

She glanced at her clock on her dashboard. Right on time. The sooner she went in, the sooner the meter would start ticking and the sooner she could leave. As she let herself out of the car and approached the restaurant, she rehearsed her preamble about bad timing and leaving early and being sorry to waste his time.

Wait. What was his name?

Oh, great. In the haze of her hurt and fury, she hadn't even asked Jake for the guy's name. He should've told her that up front. She thought about texting Jake to ask, but she really didn't want contact with him right now.

The way she felt right now was proof-positive that she needed distance. She didn't want to hate him. The only way she could stop that or any more damage from happening was to let her wounds heal. Right now, contact with Jake only tore them deeper.

She took a deep breath and squared her shoulders. She centered herself by reminding herself that the hapless, nameless man who should be waiting for her in the bar would not bear the brunt of her sorrow.

The floor-to-ceiling doors that opened onto the sidewalk in front of the bar were open. A few of the outside bistro tables were occupied, but nobody looked as if he might be waiting for a blind date. Anna circumvented the hostess stand, where Emily would be if she was indeed working tonight, and entered the bar via the open sidewalk doors.

The bar was virtually empty, save for a man and a woman making eyes at each other at a cozy corner table and four middle-aged women who occupied a four-top. Okay, so he wasn't an early bird. She pushed the button on her phone: six forty-six. Their reservation wasn't until seven. So technically she was early…as Jake had suggested.

What if her mystery date didn't show until seven?

So not only was it an inconvenience, it was awkward. *Now what?*

Anna turned in a circle for one more look to make sure she hadn't inadvertently missed him. She hadn't. Great.

She decided to sit at the bar and order a cup of tea—chamomile tea. She couldn't drink coffee because that was too much caffeine too late in the day, and she was already wound up as it was. She certainly didn't want to order a glass of wine because that would send the wrong message. When the guy arrived, she would simply tell him there had been a miscommunication and she had to leave at seven o'clock.

If she were thinking about Jake, she would want to strangle him. But she wasn't thinking about him. Nope, not at all. He was the furthest person from her mind.

The bartender had just brought her tea—she felt a little silly sitting at a bar drinking chamomile tea…but who cared? The bartender had just placed it in front of her when she heard Emily say, "Oh, my gosh, there you are. How did I not see you when you passed the hostess stand?"

That was an odd choice of words.

"How did you know I'd be here to even walk past the hostess stand?"

Emily opened her mouth to say something but then closed it quickly and glanced up at the ceiling, before she said, "I don't know what you're talking about. But I have something to show you, so come with me."

"What? No, Emily. I'm meeting somebody and, well, it's a long story, but this is not a good time. I just got my tea, and you know if I step away for even a second, my date will arrive."

"Hey, Porter," Emily said to the bartender, "watch my sister's tea for her, okay? If someone shows up looking for her, tell him she'll be right back."

Emily winked at him. She actually winked. But that wasn't the only thing that was odd. First of all, she hadn't said anything about Anna being on a date tonight after she'd had to come rescue her last night, and completely let slide the fact that Anna was drinking *chamomile tea* at a bar. God, the mileage she could've gotten out of that one.

Instead, she was all but pulling Anna off the bar stool and herding her toward the dining room.

Then the cherry on top of all the prior weirdness happened when Emily stopped suddenly and turned to her. "Look, don't be difficult tonight." She looked deadly serious. "Just go with this. Trust me, you'll thank me later."

"What?"

Emily gave an exasperated shake of her head and continued leading Anna out of the bar, across the entry and into the dining room.

What the heck was Anna supposed to say to a warning like that? When Emily got serious, which wasn't very often, she always meant business.

So what was going on?

Whatever it was, Anna decided to heed her sister's advice and just go with it.

Emily paused in front of the door to the private dining room. It was closed, but the room was partitioned by a wall with dark wood wainscoting on the bottom and leaded, beveled glass on top. The glass was fogged to give the diners privacy. Anna could see a flickering light coming from the other side, but she couldn't see who was inside.

The sudden frightening thought that the mystery man was somehow in cahoots with Jake—and had gotten her sister involved to trick her into having dinner—nearly had her hyperventilating.

Well, she wouldn't stay. He couldn't make her. And neither could Jake.

Fifteen-minute rules still applied, and she pulled out her phone, clicked the button and saw that the guy had exactly five minutes.

He can always take home a doggie bag. Give her meal to Jake, the louse. She'd made it perfectly clear she would only stay for fifteen minutes and then they'd agreed that Jake would never fix her up on a blind date again.

Would he really go to these lengths to win this absurd bet between them?

Anna didn't have time to ponder it because all of a sudden Emily threw her arms around her and said, "I am so happy for you."

Then she opened the door to the private dining room, grabbed her hand and tugged her inside.

It took a moment for Anna to register what was happening because the room was filled with red roses and candlelight and Jake was there and he was thanking her sister...for her help?

Then, after Emily left the room and shut the door behind her, he said, "God, you can be so difficult sometimes. I thought you weren't going to come."

"What are you doing? Jake, what's going on?"

They were the only two in the room. There was no mystery man and now Jake was reaching for her hand.

"I've tried twice now to tell you something important, but we keep getting interrupted. So, I figured I needed to go to drastic measures to get you alone.

"Anna, I'm your date. I'm the one. You're the one. That has become so clear to me since you've been back in Celebration. I guess sometimes it takes a lifetime to see that the love of your life has been right in front of you all along."

A peculiar humming began sounding in Anna's ears and her knees threatened to buckle beneath her. Was this really happening?

"I lost you once to a man who didn't deserve you, and I'd be an idiot to let you get away again."

Was he saying he wanted a *commitment*? *But Jake didn't, not the kind she needed.*

But maybe she needed to stop overthinking it. Stop making everything so blasted heavy and just go with it.

She loved him. She'd been in love with him her entire life. So what was the problem? Marriage hadn't given her the happily-ever-after she'd expected. So, just—

But then Jake was down on one knee and he had a small black box in his hand.

"I love you, Anna. I don't want another day to go by that I don't wake up and see your face first thing when I open my eyes. Will you do me the honor of being my wife and building a family with me? If you say yes, I promise I will make sure you have no regrets."

With tears streaming down her face, Anna was so choked up that all she could do was nod, but that was enough of a go-ahead for Jake—her mystery man, the last man she'd ever date, the one man she'd spend the rest of her life with—to take the ring from the box and slip it on her finger.

The gorgeous, classic round diamond sparkled in the candlelight as if it were celebrating with them. The sight of it on her finger and her hand in Jake's was instantly sobering.

"I love you so much," she said.

He pulled her into a deep kiss, the magic of which was only interrupted by Emily's voice. "So, I gather she said yes?"

Tears glinted in her sister's eyes.

"I did. I don't think I've ever been this happy."

Emily put her hands on her hips. "Sorry, but I have

to ask. If you two are marrying each other, who won the crazy bet?"

"We both did," Anna and Jake answered together.

* * * * *

SPECIAL EXCERPT FROM

*McKenzie Shaw works harder than anyone as the
mayor of her hometown, Haven Point. But all of her
hard work might be for nothing when her
long-ago crush, Ben Kilpatrick, shows up again,
about to wreak havoc in Haven Point—and on
McKenzie's heart.*

Read on for a sneak preview of
REDEMPTION BAY,
the latest book in New York Times *bestselling author
RaeAnne Thayne's heartwarming series,*
HAVEN POINT.
On sale now!

THIS WAS HER favorite kind of Haven Point evening.

McKenzie Shaw locked the front door of her shop, Point Made Flowers and Gifts. The day had been long and hectic, filled with customers and orders, which was wonderful, but also plenty of unavoidable mayoral business.

She was tired and wanted to stretch out on the terrace or her beloved swing, with her feet up and something cool at her elbow. The image beckoned but the sweetness of the view in front of her made her pause.

"Hold on," she said to Paprika, her cinnamon standard poodle. The dog gave her a long-suffering look but settled next to the bench in front of the store.

McKenzie sat and reached a hand down to pet Rika's curly hair. A few sailboats cut through the stunning blue waters of Lake Haven, silvery and bright in the fading light, with the rugged, snowcapped mountains as a backdrop.

She didn't stop nearly often enough to soak in the beautiful view or enjoy the June evening air, tart and clean from the mighty fir and pines growing in abundance around the lake.

A tourist couple walked past holding hands and eating gelato cones from Carmela's, their hair backlit into golden halos by the setting sun. From a short distance away, she could hear children laughing and shrieking as they played on the beach at the city park, and the alluring scent of grilling steak somewhere close by made her stomach grumble.

She loved every season here on the lake but the magnificent Haven Point summers were her favorite—especially lazy summer evenings filled with long shadows and spectacular sunsets.

Kayaking on the lake, watching children swim out to the floating docks, seeing old-timers in ancient boats casting gossamer lines out across the water. It was all part of the magic of Haven Point's short summer season.

The town heavily depended on the influx of tourists during the summer, though it didn't come close to the crowds enjoyed by the larger city to the north, Shelter Springs—especially since the Haven Point Inn burned down just before Christmas and had yet to be rebuilt.

Shelter Springs had more available lodging, more restaurants, more shopping—as well as more problems with parking, traffic congestion and crime, she reminded herself.

"Evening, Mayor," Mike Bailey called, waving as

he rumbled past the store in the gorgeous old blue '57 Chevy pickup he'd restored.

She waved back, then nodded to Luis Ayala, locking up his insurance agency across the street.

A soft, warm feeling of contentment seeped through her. This was her town, these were her people. She was part of it, just like the Redemption Mountains across the lake. She had fought to earn that sense of belonging since the day she showed up, a lost, grieving, bewildered girl.

She had worked hard to earn the respect of her friends and neighbors. The chance to serve as the mayor had never been something she sought but she had accepted the challenge willingly. It wasn't about power or influence—not that one could find much of either in a small town like Haven Point. She simply wanted to do anything she could to make a difference in her community. She wanted to think she was serving with honor and dignity, but she was fully aware there were plenty in town who might disagree.

Her stomach growled, louder this time. That steak smelled as if it was charred to perfection. Too bad she didn't know who was grilling it or she might just stop by to say hello. McKenzie was briefly tempted to stop in at Serrano's or even grab a gelato of her own at Carmela's—stracciatella, her particular favorite—but she decided she would be better off taking Rika home.

"Come on, girl. Let's go."

The dog jumped to her feet, all eager, lanky grace, and McKenzie gripped the leash and headed off.

She lived not quite a mile from her shop downtown

and she and Rika both looked forward all day to this evening walk along the trail that circled the lake.

As she walked, she waved at people walking, biking, driving, even boating past when the shoreline came into view. It was quite a workout for her arm but she didn't mind. Each wave was another reminder that this was her town and she loved it.

"Let's grill some chicken when we get home," she said aloud to Rika, whose tongue lolled out with appropriate enthusiasm.

Talking to her dog again. Not a good sign but she decided it was too beautiful an evening to worry about her decided lack of any social life to speak of. Town council meetings absolutely didn't count.

WHEN SHE REACHED her lakeside house, however, she discovered a luxury SUV with California plates in the driveway of the house next to hers, with a boat trailer and gleaming wooden boat attached.

Great.

Apparently someone had rented the Sloane house.

Normally she would be excited about new neighbors but in this case, she knew the tenants would only be temporary. Since moving to Shelter Springs, Carole Sloane-Hall had been renting out the house she'd received as a settlement in her divorce for a furnished vacation rental. Sometimes people stayed for a week or two, sometimes only a few days.

It was a lovely home, probably one of the most luxurious lakefront rentals within the city limits. Though not large, it had huge windows overlooking the lake, a wide flagstone terrace and a semiprivate boat dock—

which, unfortunately, was shared between McKenzie's own property and Carole's rental house.

She wouldn't let it spoil her evening, she told herself. Usually the renters were very nice people, quiet and polite. She generally tried to act as friendly and welcoming as possible.

It wouldn't bother her at all except the two properties had virtually an open backyard because both needed access to the shared dock, with only some landscaping between the houses that ended several yards from the high watermark. Sometimes she found the lack of privacy a little disconcerting, with strangers temporarily living next door, but Carole assured her she planned to put the house on the market at the end of the summer. With everything else McKenzie had to worry about, she had relegated the vacation rental situation next door to a distant corner of her brain.

New neighbors or not, though, she still adored her own house. She had purchased it two years earlier and still felt a little rush of excitement when she unlocked the front door and walked over the threshold.

Over those two years, she had worked hard to make it her own, sprucing it up with new paint, taking down a few walls and adding one in a better spot. The biggest expense had been for the renovated master bath, which now contained a huge claw-foot tub, and the new kitchen with warm travertine countertops and the intricately tiled backsplash she had done herself.

This was hers and she loved every inch of it, almost more than she loved her little store downtown.

She walked through to the back door and let Rika off her leash. Though the yard was only fenced on one side, just as the Sloane house was fenced on the corresponding outer property edge, Rika was well trained and never left the yard.

Her cell phone rang as she was throwing together a quick lemon-tarragon marinade for the chicken.

Some days, she wanted to grab her kayak, paddle out to the middle of Lake Haven—where it was rumored to be so deep, the bottom had never been truly charted—and toss the stupid thing overboard.

This time when she saw the caller ID, she smiled, wiped her hands on a dish towel and quickly answered. "Hey, Devin."

"Hey, sis. I can't believe you're holding out on me! Come on. Doesn't your favorite sister get to be among the first to hear?"

She tucked the phone in her shoulder and returned to cutting the lemon for the marinade as she mentally reviewed her day for anything spill-worthy to her sister.

The store had been busy enough. She had busted the doddering and not-quite-right Mrs. Anglesey for trying to walk out of the store without paying for the pretty hand-beaded bracelet she'd tried on when she came into the store with her daughter.

But that sort of thing was a fairly regular occurrence whenever Beth and her mother came into the store and was handled easily enough, with flustered apologies from Beth and that baffled "what did I do wrong?" look from poor Mrs. Anglesey.

She didn't think Devin would be particularly interested in that or the great commission she'd earned by selling one of the beautiful carved horses an artist friend made in the woodshop behind his house to a tourist from Maine.

And then there was the pleasant encounter with Mr. Twitchell, but she doubted that was what her sister meant.

"Sorry. You lost me somewhere. I can't think of any news I have worth sharing."

"Seriously? You didn't think I would want to know that Ben Kilpatrick is back in town?"

The knife slipped from her hands and she narrowly avoided chopping the tip of her finger off. A greasy, angry ball formed in her stomach.

Ben Kilpatrick. The only person on earth she could honestly say she despised. She picked up the knife and stabbed it through the lemon, wishing it was his cold, black heart.

"You're joking," she said, though she couldn't imagine what her sister would find remotely funny about making up something so outlandish and horrible.

"True story," Devin assured her. "I heard it from Betty Orton while I was getting gas. Apparently he strolled into the grocery store a few hours ago, casual as a Sunday morning, and bought what looked to be at least a week's worth of groceries. She said he didn't look very happy to be back. He just frowned when she welcomed him back."

"It's a mistake. That's all. She mistook him for someone else."

"That's what I said, but Betty assured me she's known him all his life and taught him in Sunday school three years in a row and she's not likely to mistake him for someone else."

"I won't believe it until I see him," she said. "He hates Haven Point. That's fairly obvious, since he's done his best to drive our town into the ground."

"Not actively," Devin, who tended to see the good in just about everyone, was quick to point out.

"What's the difference? By completely ignoring the property he inherited after his father died, he accomplished the same thing as if he'd walked up and down Lake Street, setting a torch to the whole downtown."

She picked up the knife and started chopping the fresh tarragon with quick, angry movements. "You know how hard it's been the last five years since he inherited to keep tenants in the downtown businesses. Haven Point is dying because of one person. Ben Kilpatrick."

If she had only one goal for her next four years as mayor, she dreamed of revitalizing a town whose lifeblood was seeping away, business by business.

When she was a girl, downtown Haven Point had been bustling with activity, a magnet for everyone in town, with several gift and clothing boutiques for both men and women, restaurants and cafés, even a downtown movie theater.

She still ached when she thought of it, when she looked around at all the empty storefronts and the ramshackle buildings with peeling paint and broken shutters.

"It's his fault we've lost so many businesses and nothing has moved in to replace them. I mean, why go to all the trouble to open a business," she demanded, "if the landlord is going to be completely unresponsive and won't fix even the most basic problems?"

"You don't have to sell it to me, Kenz. I know. I went to your campaign rallies, remember?"

"Right. Sorry." It was definitely one of her hot buttons. She loved Haven Point and hated seeing its decline—much like old Mrs. Anglesey, who had once been an elegant, respected, contributing member of the community and now could barely get around even with her daughter's help and didn't remember whether she had paid for items in the store.

"It wasn't really his fault anyway. He hired an incompetent crook of a property manager who was supposed to be taking care of things. It wasn't Ben's fault the man embezzled from him and didn't do the necessary upkeep to maintain the buildings."

"Oh, come on. Ben Kilpatrick is the chief operating officer for one of the most successful, fastest-growing companies in the world. You think he didn't know what was going on? If he had bothered to care, he would have paid more attention."

This was an argument she and Devin had had before. "At some point, you're going to have to let go," her sister said calmly. "Ben doesn't own any part of Haven Point now. He sold everything to Aidan Caine last year—which makes his presence in town even more puzzling. Why would he come back *now*, after all these years? It would seem to me, he has even *less* reason to show his face in town now."

McKenzie still wasn't buying the rumor that Ben had actually returned. He had been gone since he was seventeen years old. He didn't even come back for Joe Kilpatrick's funeral five years earlier—though she, for one, wasn't super surprised about that since Joe had been a bastard to everyone in town and especially to his only surviving child.

"It doesn't make any sense. What possible reason would he have to come back now?"

"I don't know. Maybe he's here to make amends. Did you ever think of that?"

How could he ever make amends for what he had done to Haven Point—not to mention shattering all her girlish illusions?

Of course, she didn't mention that to Devin as she tossed the tarragon into the lemon juice while her sister continued speculating about Ben's motives for coming back to town.

Her sister probably had no idea about McKenzie's ridiculous crush on Ben, that when she was younger, she had foolishly considered him her ideal guy. Just thinking about it now made her cringe.

Yes, he had been gorgeous enough. Vivid blue eyes, long sooty eyelashes, the old clichéd chiseled jaw—not to mention that lock of sun-streaked brown hair that always seemed to be falling into his eyes, just begging for the right girl to push it back, like Belle did to the Prince after the Beast in her arms suddenly materialized into him.

Throw in that edge of pain she always sensed in him and his unending kindness and concern for his sickly younger sister and it was no wonder her thirteen-year-old self—best friends with that same sister—used to pine for him to notice her, despite the four-year difference in their ages.

It was so stupid, she didn't like admitting it, even to herself. All that had been an illusion, obviously. He might have been sweet and solicitous to Lily but that was his only redeeming quality. His actions these past five years had proved that, over and over.

Through the open kitchen window, she heard Rika start barking fiercely, probably at some poor hapless chipmunk or squirrel that dared venture into her territory.

"I'd better go," she said to Devin. "Rika's mad at something."

"Yeah, I've got to go, too. Looks like the Shelter Springs ambulance is on its way with a cardiac patient."

"Okay. Good luck. Go save a life."

Her sister was a dedicated, caring doctor at Lake Haven Hospital, as passionate about her patients as McKenzie was about their town.

"Let me know if you hear anything down at city hall about why Ben Kilpatrick has come back to our fair city after all these years."

"Sure. And then maybe you can tell me why you're so curious."

She could almost hear the shrug in Devin's voice. "Are you kidding me? It's not every day a gorgeous playboy billionaire comes to town."

And that was the crux of the matter. Somehow it seemed wholly unfair, a serious karmic calamity, that he had done so well for himself after he left town. If she had her way, he would be living in the proverbial van down by the river—or at least in one of his own dilapidated buildings.

Rika barked again and McKenzie hurried to the back door that led onto her terrace. She really hoped it wasn't a skunk. They weren't uncommon in the area, especially not this time of year. Her dog had encountered one the week before on their morning run on a favorite mountain trail and it had taken her three baths in the magic solution she'd found on the internet before she could allow Rika back into the house.

Her dog wasn't in the yard, she saw immediately. Now that she was outside, she realized the barking was more excited and playful than upset. All the more reason to hope she wasn't trying to make nice with some odiferous little friend.

"Come," she called. "Inside."

The dog bounded through a break in the bushes between the house next door, followed instantly by another dog—a beautiful German shepherd with classic markings.

She had been right. Rika *had* been making friends. She and the German shepherd looked tight as ticks, tails wagging as they raced exuberantly around the yard.

The dog must belong to the new renters of the Sloane house. Carole would pitch a royal fit if she knew they had a dog over there. McKenzie knew it was strictly prohibited.

Now what was she supposed to do?

A man suddenly walked through the gap in landscaping. He had brown hair, but a sudden piercing ray of the setting sun obscured his features more than that.

She *really* didn't want a confrontation with the man, especially not on a Friday night when she had been so looking forward to a relaxing night at home. She supposed she could just call Carole or the property management company and let them deal with the situation.

That seemed a cop-out since Carole had asked her to keep an eye on the place.

She forced a smile and approached the dog's owner. "Hi. Good evening. You must be renting the place from Carole. I'm McKenzie Shaw. I live next door. Rika, that dog you're playing catch with, is mine."

The man turned around and the pleasant evening around her seemed to go dark and still as she took in brown sun-streaked hair, steely blue eyes, chiseled jaw.

Her stomach dropped as if somebody had just picked her up and tossed her into the cold lake.

Ben Kilpatrick. Here. Staying in the house next door.

So much for her lovely evening at home.

* * * * *

Don't miss
REDEMPTION BAY by RaeAnne Thayne,
available July 2015 wherever
HQN Books are sold.
www.HQNBooks.com

COMING NEXT MONTH FROM

H HARLEQUIN®

SPECIAL EDITION

Available July 21, 2015

#2419 Do You Take This Maverick?
Montana Mavericks: What Happened at the Wedding?
by Marie Ferrarella

Claire Strickland is in mommy mode, caring for her baby girl, Bekka. She doesn't have time for nights on the town...*unlike* her estranged husband, Levi Wyatt. The carousing cowboy wants to prove he's man enough to keep his family together, but can he show the woman he loves that their family is truly meant to be?

#2420 One Night in Weaver...
Return to the Double C • by Allison Leigh

Psychologist Hayley Templeton has always pictured herself with an Ivy League boyfriend, but she can't seem to get sexy security guard Seth Banyon out of her mind. Overwhelmed with work, Hayley turns to Seth for relief in more ways than one. She soon finds there's more heart and passion to this seeming Average Joe than she ever could have imagined.

#2421 The Boss, the Bride & the Baby
Brighton Valley Cowboys • by Judy Duarte

Billionaire Jason Rayburn is back home on his family's Texas ranch, looking to renovate and sell off the property. So he brings in lovely Juliana Bailey to help him clean up the Leaning R. Juliana is reluctant to work with irresistibly handsome Jason, who's the son of an infamous local businessman. Besides, she has a baby secret she's trying to keep—at the risk of her heart!

#2422 The Cowboy's Secret Baby
The Mommy Club • by Karen Rose Smith

One night with bull rider Ty Conroy gave Marissa Lopez an amazing gift—her son, Jordan. She never expected to see the freewheeling cowboy again, but Ty is back in town after a career-ending injury forced him to start over. Both Marissa and Ty are reluctant to trust one another, but doing so might just lasso them the greatest prize of all—family!

#2423 A Reunion and a Ring
Proposals & Promises • by Gina Wilkins

To ponder a proposal, Jenny Baer retreats to her childhood haunt, a cabin in the Arkansas hills. To her surprise, she's met there by her college sweetheart, ex-cop Gavin Locke. Years ago, their passion blazed brightly until Jenny convinced herself she wanted a more secure future. Can these long-lost lovers heal past wounds...and create the future together they'd always wanted?

#2424 Following Doctor's Orders
Texas Rescue • by Caro Carson

Dr. Brooke Brown works tirelessly as an ER doctor. She does her best to ignore too-handsome playboy firefighter Zach Bisho, who threatens her concentration. But not even Brooke can resist, soon succumbing to his charm, and a fling soon turns into love...even as Zach discovers his adorable long-lost daughter. Despite past hurts, Brooke and Zach soon find that there's nowhere they'd rather be than in each other's arms...forever!

YOU CAN FIND MORE INFORMATION ON UPCOMING HARLEQUIN® TITLES, FREE EXCERPTS AND MORE AT WWW.HARLEQUIN.COM.

HSECNM0715

REQUEST YOUR FREE BOOKS!
2 FREE NOVELS PLUS 2 FREE GIFTS!

♦ HARLEQUIN®

SPECIAL EDITION
Life, Love & Family

"You don't mind if I see her?" he asked uncertainly.

"No, I don't mind," Claire answered in the same quiet
voice. She gestured toward the baby lying in the portable
playpen. "Go on, it's okay. Since Bekka lights up whenever you walk into a room, maybe it might be a good
thing for her if you spent a little time with our little girl."

"Thanks," Levi said to her with feeling. Then he slanted
another look toward Claire—a longer one as he tried to
puzzle things out—and asked, "How do you feel about
my spending time with her mother?"

Claire arched one eyebrow as she regarded him. "I
wouldn't push it if I were you, Levi," she warned.

He raised his hands in a sign of complete surrender.
"Message received. You don't need to say another word,
Claire. My question is officially rescinded," he told her.

And then, because he prided himself on always being truthful with Claire, he added, "I'm a patient man. I can wait until you decide to change your mind about that."

Because he had really left her no recourse if she was to save face, Claire told him, "I don't think there's enough patience in the whole world for that."

"We'll see," Levi said softly, more to himself than to her. "We'll see."

Claire gave no indication that she had overheard him. But she had.

And something very deep inside her warmed to his words.

Don't miss
DO YOU TAKE THIS MAVERICK?
by Marie Ferrarella, available August 2015 wherever
Harlequin® Special Edition books and ebooks are sold.

www.Harlequin.com

THE WORLD IS BETTER WITH

Romance

Harlequin has everything from contemporary, passionate and heartwarming to suspenseful and inspirational stories.

Whatever your mood, we have a romance just for you!

Connect with us to find your next great read, special offers and more.

 /HarlequinBooks

@HarlequinBooks

www.HarlequinBlog.com

www.Harlequin.com/Newsletters

HARLEQUIN®

A *Romance* FOR EVERY MOOD™

www.Harlequin.com